It Happened in Essex 2

Basildon Writers' Group

ISBN: 9798863285924

Editorial: Wendy Ogilvie Editorial Services
Interior design: Janet Watts

Basildon Hospital Radio – BHR 87.7 FM

Basildon Hospital Radio volunteers provide quality entertainment, news and information to patients 365 days a year, keeping them connected to the outside world. During this past year, it has been difficult to raise donations, so we are very grateful that the Basildon Writers' Group is coming to our rescue.

They have launched "It Happened in Essex 2", containing stories written by fourteen local writers, with all the proceeds being given to BHR87.7 (Basildon Hospital Radio). The hospital radio is run by local volunteers. We fund it ourselves and rely heavily on donations to pay the bills and keep the equipment in working order.

Our wonderful volunteers are music enthusiasts but are also people-orientated. Once, during a Vera Lynn theme on one of the wards, I was mistaken for the lady herself and asked to sing. "The White Cliffs of Dover". Not wanting to let anyone down, I obliged, much to the amusement of the other patients and nurses.

We regularly visit the wards and for some patients, a BHR volunteer may be the only visitor they have all day.

I am asking you to support us by buying a copy of this wonderful book, written with love and devotion by members of the Basildon Writers' Group. And please recommend it to your friends and family.

Many thanks,

Jacqui James

Chairman BHR87.7 FM (Basildon Hospital Radio)

If you enjoy our book and want to encourage others to buy it and support Basildon Hospital Radio (BHR), please consider reviewing *It Happened in Essex 2* in Amazon and/ or Goodreads. An honest review will help boost sales and therefore donations to BHR.

Also, please consider buying the first *It Happened in Essex* book which you can find on Amazon, here https://mybook.to/ItHappenedInEssex and consider reviewing that, too.

Thank you for your support,
from Basildon Writers' Group and Basildon Hospital Radio

Contents

PART ONE

It Never Occurred to Me – By Rob Coke

I passed that fateful spot on so many occasions, and yet it never occurred to me.

As a child, I wandered the abandoned structures at the Stow Maries Aerodrome at my leisure. The remnants of a time period elapsed generations before I was born. Crumbling architecture, overgrown wilderness, land littered with lakes – unwanted gifts from the Luftwaffe, a paradise for a young boy to roam and play. I would sprint through the lengthy grass which enveloped me, searching frantically for the remnants of one more forgotten bygone edifice. If I found one, some more intact than others, the overwhelming fascination with the connection to its past would wash over me, feeling its walls, searching its floor for some trinket, imagination running wild for what this place once achieved, what purpose its residents once had, what life here must have been like. I felt truly blessed that I was local enough to experience this time machine on my doorstep, and thankful in hindsight for how influential it was on developing my passion for history, which lasts to this day.

And as I passed that fateful spot, once again, it never

occurred to me.

As I grew older, the site began to develop. Interest soared like the planes which once circled above; articles were published about it, workmen poured in, a buzz forming around the exciting prospect that this glorious place, the last of its kind, the most intact and unspoilt aerodrome from the First World War, was to be restored to its former glory.

My father knew someone who was involved with this; time has taken his name from my memory. We visited with him to see the changes, and how incredible it was! Those dilapidated, disastrous playhouses of mine were becoming the living, breathing monuments that they deserved to be. I saw many a structure which I had never discovered as a boy and took a childlike pleasure in miniature expeditions to these as well. The two elders took pleasure in my own, overjoyed that the next generation was to develop as much an interest in the site as themselves. I went home that day with an intense nostalgia for those bygone days of my adventures.

And as I passed that fateful spot, once again, it never occurred to me.

By now, I was well into my teens. My high school took me on visits there. Sure, a tree still grew from the water tower, dereliction surrounded us from the outer buildings, but it seemed surreal. I swung the new wooden door open to the airmen's mess, to be greeted with the fragrance of fresh paint, the splendour of decoration, the roughness of the raw brick which I remembered so vividly upon my younger fingers replaced with wooden furnishings. I sat down to tea with the pianola tinkling a faint melody in the corner. It was as I expected it to be all those years ago, my mind wandering to the days where I sat here with all these niceties removed, wondering if I ever believed back then if I would ever come again to find it in such a fine, renovated condition. To say that

I was impressed by what had been done to the place so far would have been an understatement.

I knew that aircraft would be here from time to time, but at this stage in my life, I was yet to see one of these fine, ancient warbirds soaring overhead. Perhaps it was bad timing by the school, perhaps they couldn't afford a visit on a fly-day or couldn't be bothered. Yet I was so blessed to witness what I had just experienced, that it mattered little. The time for that was sure to come, I thought, just like the time for the other buildings to be in the same shape as this one would, rising from their forgotten pasts like Phoenixes from the ashes. I went home that day with a great sense of optimism for the future of a place I held so dear.

And as I passed that fateful spot, once again, it never occurred to me.

A few more years had passed, and once again the opportunity to return came upon me. I had a lonely night, home alone, my parents having vanished for the evening. My father had received an invite to dine with his boss at Hylands House, my mother obviously accompanying him. The aerodrome played a key role at this charity dinner; a Sopwith Camel greeted them upon entry and, for the fee of ten pounds, one could enter a raffle. My father won a guided tour of the site for two, plus afternoon tea at the airmen's mess. He chose to take me, and ecstatically, I returned to the location which I had loved for so long.

The rain pummelled us as we strolled up the track to meet the volunteer who would show us around. The wind howled like the aircraft which once flooded the skies above us. Yet determined, we perused the site with the gentleman of incredible knowledge, unlocking secrets which the childhood version of me would have given the world to know. Tiny, obscure details, historical accuracy of the highest degree, that overwhelming fascination from years gone by returning strong. My dream to see some of the aircraft came true as we wandered the recently erected hangars, each one being listed off one by one with equal detail to the other matters presented by the chap earlier on, such as the captivating museum. And of course, more of those structures from days of yore in brand new glory days, the same sensation as that school day at the airmen's mess flooding back.

Despite the Somme-like soil, my muddied boots held as I passed that fateful spot, this time accompanied by the volunteer, who halted me, and began his next bombardment of fascinating facts. His finger extended through the downpour, towards a gap in the greenery, which appeared to be the fateful spot in question, and he made it occur to me.

'That is known as Milburn's Gap,' he explained. 'Lieutenant Cyril Milburn died there in April 1918. His Sopwith Camel stalled as he passed the gap, and he went up in the fireball with it. He was one of ten men from here who lost their lives.'

It is always the personal aspects of history which have gripped me, and that is one of the stories that has always stuck. The volunteers all felt a deep connection to the gentleman who perished, and it also made me think about my own family. My great grandparents lived locally and my great grandfather drove an ambulance – perhaps there was a connection? Another great grandfather served locally during the war – perhaps they knew one another? Oh, if only they were still alive to ask! One would be mistaken to think that disasters in times such as those happened far away, but in fact, they are close by, both physically, and metaphorically to those affected. It was an aspect which flew miles over my head in those previous years of endless joy, and I left that day sombre as I wandered once again through the driving rain, towards our

4

car and the comforts of home. It felt necessary to feel such a way, and I was glad of it, being an aspect so neglected in my memory. The grounding in reality forever changed how I interpreted the past.

Nowadays, I'm a living historian. Many more years had passed by before my group received an offer to attend Stow Maries. I once again found myself on the track to the aerodrome. This time I was not wandering, nor sauntering, nor rushing around with feverous excitement. I had a uniform on my back, hob-nailed boots on my feet and a rifle in my hands, marching to a steady beat on the approach, with the nostalgia brimming beneath my cap. My dream of seeing the aircraft fly came true as our column was buzzed by a squadron of biplanes at a ridiculously low altitude. So many more of those beloved buildings glowed radiantly as I marched by. I spent the weekend educating the public on history, partaking in parades and displays, as well as our normal interaction with visitors, imparting my feelings from years gone by into the next generation, with the hope that they would get that glimmer of fascination which I had – the torch being passed on.

On the Saturday evening, I entered the airmen's mess once again, this time to a jovial atmosphere. As I was renowned for being musically talented, I struck up some songs on the request of the aerodrome's chief executive officer, and before I knew it, one of the best nights out I have ever experienced unfolded. Each unit, centred around their own table, sang the tunes familiar to them, forming the most energetic of environments. A sergeant (whom I shall spare the embarrassment of naming) sang a rendition of 'Hold your Hand Out, Naughty Boy' whilst incredibly inebriated to the delight of all. By the end of the night, we were informed that this was the first time since 1919, when the site was decommissioned, that the airmen's mess was used for its intended purpose. Once again, a childhood dream had come true, to understand what life was like here, and this time it wasn't explained, it was experienced first-hand.

The evening ended with the chief executive officer offering words of remembrance regarding the ten who perished here to calm the atmosphere down. One could've heard a pin drop at his speech. Perhaps our night was just like the last, fateful nights that the heroes of the aerodrome experienced before never returning. I hope that they all shared in the same happiness that we did. We staggered to our billets, bedded down for the night, and we all looked back hoping that we had done them proud. I hoped that they would appreciate our presence, our educating the public on their lives and their aerodrome, and the portrayal of their history to the people of Essex. I like to think that they would be smiling to see their aerodrome restored, and wishing that they could partake in the festivities that took over a century to materialise.

Who knows when I'll next return, and what will come of it. My experience with the Stow Maries Aerodrome has been quite the journey, and I hope that this is just the beginning.

Heaven in Herongate – By Menderes Doğan

There she is again. In her little garden, on her own as usual. One hand is in the pot, and the other is holding a plant. She's giving me the 'daggers' again. She doesn't worry about the possibility I'll confront her.

What if I say, 'Oi, you old bag, who are you looking at?'

But she knows I won't say anything. She knows I'll take my eyes off her as soon as I meet her hostile stare. She knows me well. I feel like a fool that I waved at her once. Just to prove I'm a friendly person, and she doesn't need to stare at me like she does. But she ignored me and carried on staring. I don't know much about her apart from the fact that she is my neighbour who lives on the corner of my street. She seems to love gardening and staring at people.

One day, I was walking home with my fiancée and saw her in her little piece of heaven. Heaven on steps, I should say. It was her front garden, no grass, just dozens of pots all over the four large steps. She was sitting on something. Like an upside-down bucket or a little stool. She always sits; I've never seen her working standing up. I think she has a problem with her legs. She must have been either potting up a new plant or replanting some older ones.

Anyway, I was walking home with my fiancée. The old lady looked at us. She did not take her eyes off us from the second we appeared at the corner of our street until we walked past her home. My fiancée has been living here for some time. I only moved in with her a couple of years ago. It wasn't long after I moved to Herongate, Essex and started to do the night shift at the warehouse. I knew it was putting pressure on our relationship. My fiancée worked as a shop assistant in the daytime, and I worked at night. We hardly saw each other.

It was OK when I first moved in. We felt like we each still had our own personal space, but then reality hit, and we realised we were drifting apart. As I said, because I have been working different hours, I hadn't realised the old woman existed. Short, curly, grey hair that was always scruffy. A sinister face. You know what I mean? You can't miss the hostility and meanness behind those eyeballs. I asked my fiancée who the woman was and why on earth she always gave the 'evils' to everyone who walked past her home.

She told me the woman, whose name was apparently Mary, had been living there for years.

'She does stare at everyone, but she's harmless. Just a little grumpy.'

Nevertheless, I had the feeling I wouldn't want to mess with her. And, I was glad to hear the old witch had a name. Now I could come up with nicknames for her. Mary the Cranky, or Scary Mary. You know what? Maybe Starey Mary will be the best.

All that summer and until mid-autumn, she was in her garden. She had some roses along the fence of her next-door neighbour. All in pots. Beautiful red and white roses. In fact, I don't even remember seeing roses as beautiful as hers. Some pinky, orange dahlias and a big, bushy red-white fuchsia are at the front of her garden along the public footpath. There were white and yellow daffodils and narcissi in the spring, then sunflowers in the autumn.

She even extended her little heaven to the other side of the footpath, which technically didn't belong to her. It was the corner of the street where the tangle of blackberry bushes grew. She must have planted those purple hollyhocks there amongst them too. Some of them were taller than me. And those honeysuckle bushes were a natural border between the wild blackberries and her heaven. I guess nobody would complain about her little extension. It looked beautiful and smelled nice. What could be better in your neighbourhood?

Herongate is a lovely little village to live in. I guess we couldn't afford to live here if my fiancée hadn't inherited the house from her parents. It would be a common mistake to associate the name of the village with the bird. I will never forget when my fiancée told me it had nothing to do with herons. She must have been fed up seeing me keep gazing at the sky and trees, looking for herons. Apparently, Heron was the name of the family who once owned Heron Hall. There is no moated hall with towers; once, it used to be on the east side of the village. But there are some nice houses with lovely little gardens here.

I remember when I was at school, one of my teachers mentioning the benefits of a beautiful garden. I don't remember what else he was talking about, but it must have been about things that make people happy, yet don't cost anything. Something that's free but also gives joy.

I recall he said, 'Imagine a friend walking out of his home to go to work. He is looking at his neighbour's beautiful garden, and what he sees makes him happy. He didn't have to spend a penny for this. Not only that, but he hasn't had to dedicate his time to making that garden beautiful. His neighbour did it by himself, for himself; with no thought to giving anyone else pleasure. Nevertheless, your friend enjoys the garden more than his neighbour because he hasn't had to do the work nor will he have the responsibility of its upkeep.'

I am sure I wasn't the only person in the area enjoying all those different colours and scents every time I walked past her house.

There was a price to be paid for the pleasure, though. I was not like the man in my teacher's example. I had to pay something for it. The price I had to pay was to suffer those daggers she was throwing at me whenever I walked past her house while she was in the garden.

I ignored her threatening looks as much as I could. But I swear I could feel her little daggers stabbing me in the back. I'm sure you know how uncomfortable it is when you feel you're being watched.

Winter came suddenly. Her little garden could not resist the plunging temperatures of the freezing nights. Everything withered and died. All those colours and heavenly smells were gone.

I tried to see the half-full glass. All that beauty had disappeared, but at least I didn't have to avoid her hostile stare as I passed by.

It was around mid-winter when I saw a woman carrying a few bags coming out of our street. She was in her forties. A short-haired brunette, wearing a brown roll-neck jumper, jeans, and a jacket with a fur collar. I offered her help and carried the bags to the car for her.

She said I was a true gentleman.

I tried to be cheeky and said, 'Oh, that means you don't know me very well.'

She smiled as I put the bags in her car boot. The bags

were filled with clothes and some ornaments.

She thanked me and said, 'Right, dangerous stranger, I have a few more bags to carry. Are you willing to help a vulnerable lady?'

I laughed and agreed to help. We walked together and turned the corner of our street. I felt a bit uneasy when we started to walk up to Starey Mary's footpath. I thought she would appear from the door or from the window and give me 'daggers'.

The woman took her key out and opened Mary's door. A really heavy, musty smell flooded out and attacked my nostrils. I realised I'd expected her house to smell as nice as her garden in the summer.

I asked her if she was Mary's relative.

She said, 'I'm her daughter … I mean, I was.' She paused, then continued once we were inside the house. 'Maybe you heard; she passed away last week.'

I said I was so sorry and gave my condolences. She went into the front room and started to put some more ornaments in a carrier bag. You know the sort of thing; little animals, fairies, and some unlit candles.

She told me they hadn't been very close, as they didn't get along well. 'Perhaps you've heard her reputation; she wasn't an easy person to get along with.'

I lied and said I'd never had a problem with her. Well, maybe I wasn't lying. I had a problem with her stare, but I'd never had a problem directly with her.

I remarked that her garden had been beautiful.

The woman stopped and looked out the window at the, now barren, garden.

'I suppose you're right. Mum's garden was beautiful. She lavished all her love to that little garden. The love she kept from … everyone.'

She turned and carried on, putting more ornaments in the

carrier bag. Suddenly she stopped and said her mother was found lying by the front room door, where I was standing. Apparently, the postman spotted her through the window and called an ambulance. A shiver ran through me at the thought of Starey Mary's body having lain where I was standing so I moved away, towards the window. I followed her to the kitchen, where she had some more bags already packed. Being in Starey Mary's house was awkward enough but having heard she'd passed away made me feel like getting out of this house as soon as possible. However, the woman was looking at me with appealing eyes. Like she was telling me, *'Come on, are you going to pick up these bags? You agreed to help,'* without saying a word.

So, I took the bags from her. She opened the front door but stopped when she saw something on the hall table. She grabbed a pair of old glasses. She looked at them with tears in her eyes and told me her mother could barely see anything in the distance without them. Then, with a sad smile, she put them in her pocket.

We put the rest of the bags in her car. I once again said how sorry I was to hear that Mary had passed away. She got in her car, drove off, and I never saw her again.

The house was sold not long after. Now, there is a young childless couple living there. They both work; I guess there's no time for gardening. They threw all the pots away. The heaven on steps is, now, just some steps.

During the spring, my eyes searched for daffodils each time I walked past that garden.

I must admit, I missed that beautiful garden. Maybe Mary was a grumpy old woman, or perhaps she simply couldn't see without her glasses, giving the impression she was glaring at people. I don't know. All I know is that I could take Mary's 'daggers' to my heart if I could see that beautiful garden again.

Bottled Revenge – By Jenny Drew

Terry Baker was excited. Tonight, he was getting his revenge.

In a few short hours, Sullivan would get payback. It was a shame Terry couldn't be there to see his face, but Terry and the young lad, Jordan, would know, and that was enough for Terry.

He hadn't known the lad long, but he'd proved himself very useful on more than one occasion. Terry knew his dad wasn't around, and figured he could step into that space.

It was thanks to Jordan that they were sitting here now, in a white van a few miles from Dagenham docks. Terry looked across at Jordan playing on his phone. He must be getting sentimental in his old age because he'd developed a bit of a soft spot for the lad.

Not wanting Jordan to catch him staring, Terry picked up the binoculars to check for the truck.

'Remind me how you came by this information again?' said Terry, putting the binoculars down.

'Eric, the geezer who drives the truck. He likes to brag a little when he's had a few,' said Jordan, going back on his phone.

'This is definitely the route he's going to take?' Terry

tapped the steering wheel impatiently.

'Yeah Terry, I followed him loads of times; he always took the same route.' Jordan rolled his eyes.

'And you know for sure that the special delivery is coming tonight?'

Jordan nodded. 'Yep, fifteen grand's worth of booze, and it'll be here tonight. According to Eric, there's also a crate of Macallan whisky, which is for Sullivan personally.'

Terry whistled. 'Macallan single malt, nice. That goes for a few hundred a bottle. Knowing it's for Sullivan personally, I might just keep that for myself. I'm quite partial to a single malt.'

'How come we're so early, anyway? We got ages yet until he's due,' said Jordan, fiddling with the music controls.

'Leave it alone, Jordan. Come on lad, you don't want to draw attention to us.'

'But we've been here ages, Terry,' said Jordan, leaning back in his chair grabbing his phone again.

'I like to get the lay of the land. If you don't plan, Jordan, then mistakes happen and then you get caught.'

'Is that how you got sent to prison before?'

'No!' Terry punched the steering wheel. 'That scumbag Sullivan grassed me up.'

'Really? You think Sullivan's a grass?' said Jordan, pulling a face.

Terry scowled. 'I know he is. His mate was banged up inside the same time I was and he told me.'

Terry didn't like this attitude of Jordan's. Why was the lad questioning him?

'What, just like that? A rival of yours just comes up and grassed up his friend?' Jordan eyed Terry.

'Let's just say he needed a little persuading, but I got it out of him in the end.' Terry smirked.

14

Jordan grabbed Terry's arm. 'Is that the geezer you did over, the one you shanked?'

Terry shoved Jordan off. The boy got too excited over nothing. 'You don't show weakness inside. If you do, you're a goner for sure.'

Terry took a deep breath. He had to remember the boy was only a teenager and couldn't control his reactions. Jordan would come good; he was sure of it.

'That's not how I would do it. I would make it nice and slow. Feed him a bottle of antifreeze and watch him die.'

'What?' Terry turned to face the boy, he wasn't sure he had heard him right, but before he could say anything, headlights lit up the road and a truck could be seen speeding towards them. A glance in the binoculars confirmed it was the one they were waiting for.

They followed from a distance. There wasn't much traffic on the road and they knew the route he would be taking.

'Jordan, open the glove compartment and hand me a balaclava. You've got yours, haven't you?'

Jordan nodded and handed one to Terry.

'Right Jordan, you remember the plan?'

Jordan tutted 'Yeah Terry, I ain't no kid, I know the plan.'

With their balaclavas in place, Terry floored the accelerator and overtook the truck. He jerked the van to the left and screeched to a stop in front of it, forcing it to hit the brakes. Terry and Jordan jumped out. Terry produced a sawn-off shot gun and waved for the driver to get out of the truck.

'On your knees.' Directed Terry to the driver.

The driver fell to his knees, visibly shaking.

'Terry man, take it easy. No need for no trouble here.'

Terry shot Jordan a warning look. 'Won't be no trouble as long as our friend here does what he's told.'

The driver looked like he wanted to speak so Terry took

the butt of the gun and knocked him unconscious. One less complication to worry about in Terry's book.

He threw Jordan some rope. 'Tie him up, and make it good.'

'Alright Terry man, don't be so uptight. I know what I'm doing.'

Terry looked at the unconscious driver and then at Jordan. 'You trying to get us caught? Stop saying my name.'

Jordan grinned 'Sorry, Terry. Won't do it again.'

'This ain't a joke, Jordan. Take it seriously.'

Jordan laughed. Terry stomped over to the truck. The boy was making him mad and he needed to be clear headed. He'd lay down the law later when they were done.

With the driver safely tied up and moved to the side of the road, Terry watched as Jordan sauntered across to the van. *That boy's too confident for his own good* he thought.

After dumping the truck in a quiet industrial estate, and moving the booze to Terry's lock up. They held on to a couple of boxes of beer and the crate of whisky and went back to Terry's flat.

'Sort out the booze, while I nip to the loo,' said Terry over his shoulder.

Terry joined Jordan in the front room. The lad had opened two of the bottles of whisky. 'Easy there Jordan. One bottle would have been enough.'

Jordan shrugged. 'It's not like its gonna go off, besides thought you could handle it?'

Terry sat down on the sofa opposite Jordan. The lad was right. No point creating an atmosphere. He'd wait 'til tomorrow to have a word with the boy, tonight they were celebrating.

He poured himself a large glass and leaned forward to clink Jordan's can 'Let's drink, we've earned it.' He took a long satisfying gulp. The scotch was like velvet liquid going down his throat. Oh yes, he was going to well and truly enjoy drinking every last drop.

Terry felt a nice buzz. The scotch was so smooth he'd drunk most of the first bottle. He looked over at Jordan and noticed he'd only drunk a couple of cans.

'Come on Jordan lad, keep up. I thought we were celebrating?'

Jordan picked up his can and chugged the contents, crushing it when it was empty.

'Good lad, can't have a lightweight as my protégé now, can we?'

'I ain't gonna be no protégé.'

'Well,' said Terry gesturing with his arms. 'I thought I could teach you a few things.'

Jordan grabbed a can and opened it, spilling some of the contents before chucking it back.

'Teach me a few things, yeah right. I'm already way ahead of you, old man.'

Terry laughed 'Still life in the old dog yet. I could teach you plenty of tricks.'

Jordan smirked and drank his beer. Terry picked up his drink and took another gulp, finishing it. As he reached for the bottle, he started seeing double, and both of them were playing musical squares. He took a deep breath and concentrated as he grabbed the bottle on the left and grinned as he made purchase. Jordan just stared.

'This scotch is some strong stuff,' said Terry, trying to lighten the mood.

He watched as Jordan leaned back in his chair, a slight smile on his lips 'Yeah definitely strong stuff I'd say, Terry.'

Terry blinked a couple of times, trying to focus. The room was spinning.

'I'm going for a slash.'

As Jordan got up and adjusted his jeans. Terry saw something flutter to the ground. He raised his hand to warn the lad but he was already disappearing out of the room.

Terry tried to stand. He was having a hard time making his legs do what he wanted them to. The room was still spinning, making Terry feel sick. He managed to get around the table before falling down and rolling on the floor. He laid there for a moment, too drunk to move. Reaching over he grabbed the item and sat up so he could look at it better.

He wondered if it was a picture of a girl Jordan liked. Grinning to himself he unfolded the photo. The images wouldn't stay still so he tried squeezing his eyes shut and opening them again. When it came into focus, Terry stared at the photo. His drunken brain couldn't understand fully but he knew he was in deep trouble.

Terry looked up as Jordan came back in the room 'You dropped this' he said, waving the photo at him. 'What you got a picture of Sullivan for?'

'Cos he's, my godfather.' Jordan said shrugging.

Terry swallowed. 'And the other man?'

'That is my dad.' Jordan said as he snatched the photo from Terry.

Terry sat there dumbfounded. The world just turned upside down and he was having a hard time thinking. He needed to think, but his brain wouldn't co-operate.

'I'm sorry Jordan, I didn't know,' Terry said hoping the boy would understand.

Jordan scoffed. 'Of course you didn't old man, you've been played, right from the start.'

Terry tried to clear his head. He needed to explain to Jordan, to make him see, how things were.

'Jordan if you could let me explain?' he started. 'Wait,

what d'you mean, from the start?' Terry asked screwing his face up in confusion.

'Was waiting for you to get out of prison. Originally, I was just gonna do you over as soon as you come out but Pat said I should wait.'

'Sullivan told you to wait?'

'Yeah, said we could get you good and proper if we plan it right.'

Terry swayed slightly. This couldn't be happening. All this time he thought he was getting revenge on Sullivan and instead it was Sullivan getting one over on him.

'So, what now?' Terry slurred. 'Is Sullivan going to arrange for me to go back to prison?'

He should have known it was too easy, but he hadn't wanted to question the lad's info. Stupid, stupid Terry he thought dejectedly.

'It's already been done.' Jordan gloated.

Maybe it was the booze but when Terry looked at Jordan, he didn't recognise the lad. This wasn't the Jordan he'd got to know over the last few months.

'Jordan, come on lad. You don't need to do this. I can't go back to prison.'

'Prison?' Jordan sneered 'You ain't going to make it back to prison, Terry.'

'You going to do me over then?'

Terry watched as Jordan walked over to the table and grabbed their drinks. Hope ballooned in his chest. Maybe it would be okay.

Jordan crouched down in front of Terry and handed him his glass. Terry took a sip, keeping his eyes on Jordan.

'You don't have to do this,' Terry said, hoping he could reach the boy.

'Told you Terry, it's already been done. You're walking

dead. Well sitting dead.' Jordan laughed.

'I don't understand, Jordan.'

He watched as Jordan got up and disappeared into the kitchen for a few minutes. He could've tried to make a run for it but he was too drunk to move.

'Did you like your scotch Terry?' he said, coming back. 'It was a special blend.'

'I know Jordan, I was there when we stole it.'

'Nah, Terry.' Jordan laughed and pulled out a white bottle. 'You might think you've been drinking Macallan but really you've been drinking this, with a bit of Macallan mixed in.'

Terry read the label. Antifreeze. The blood drained from his face.

'Jordan, you didn't?' He smiled, hoping it was some kind of joke.

'You killed my dad, Terry. Do you think I would let that go?'

The room started to spin. A gulf of pain erupted in Terry's abdomen causing him to cry out as he keeled over on his side.

'That'll be it kicking in right about now,' said Jordan.

Terry Baker watched Jordan crack open a beer and a raise a toast before he lost consciousness.

The inspiration for my fictional story was that on Thursday 7th September 2006 a lorry containing £15,000 worth of lager was hijacked in Aveley Essex. The two drivers were tied up and threatened by an armed gang. The lorry was found abandoned the next day in Dagenham and was completely empty.

The Peril of Mr Pilkins – By Pagan Field

It has been said, the grounds of the old church of St Mary, which had lain in ruin and disrepair, were cursed, while others merely hoped that were true. But it was well known locally that animals would not dare to tread there, except for the crows, who delighted in pecking through the debris of gravestones and worms – long since starved of sustenance. No one had been buried there in centuries.

It is said, all those who were involved in the excavation of the land, and the subsequent building project, experienced unexplainable phenomena, plagued by unsettling accounts of noises, visions, and voices.

But none so much as the unfortunate site manager, Mr Robert Pilkins.

One unseasonably chilly summer morning, a throng of workmen gathered in the construction yard.

'I don't know what it is about this place,' said a young apprentice while taking a deep drag on his cigarette, 'but something's not right, it feels wrong somehow, like we shouldn't be here.'

'Don't be such a pussy,' another lad jeered, but he too had felt uneasy around the site.

Work had begun on the project several days before that would see the disused grounds of St Mary transformed into a premium living space. The local council, or indeed government, had little to no regard for the living, let alone the dead, so the desecration of the church grounds paled into insignificance in the face of profit.

It was envisioned, that once complete, wealthy Londoners looking for a countryside retreat within touching distance of transport links to the big city, would flock to this previously derelict part of town and revitalise it.

It wasn't long into the construction that the men started to grumble of strange drops in temperature, of breath streaming and teeth chattering cold, or the sound of gushing water, like the babbling of a brook, though no water or rivers were known to flow through there.

Some had seen dark shadows moving across the yard, sometimes in the shape of a man, other times in the shape of a dog.

Others had heard the voice of a woman pleading or quietly sobbing.

While all the men spoke of a feeling of being watched, or as if there was someone or something standing directly behind them. Sometimes this sensation would be followed by another, of being physically touched, even pushed, to the ground.

The most disturbing account was when one of the workmen, first to arrive and eager to start the day, found a skulk of dismembered foxes strewn across the work yard. Their flame-coloured furs drenched in their innards had already begun to be picked clean by the crows. It is perhaps no surprise that that particular workman never returned to the site, and instead took up an office job in Bristol.

The site manager brushed all this off as silly superstition and as 'Any excuse not to work'. The men were cautioned to keep a lid on their stories and were threatened with dismissal should they continued to spout such gibberish.

'The old wives' tales stop here fellas; do you hear me?' He glared down at the men from the top step to his office.

Mr Pilkins was a man of sense and rationale, blissfully devoid of imagination or humour, as such creatures often are. However, his ill temper often got the better of him. Quick to anger and sullenness, he was not well liked among the other men, but he was self-assured enough not to care much for the opinions of others.

'I swear if I hear one more bullshit story about ghosts or shadows or some such bullocks, you'll not just be going home for the day, you'll be getting your p45 in the post.' He sneered.

Disgruntled, the men obeyed for fear of being kicked off the job, and so they pushed forward with the development. Nothing was going to stop the build and so things continued uninterrupted, at least for a few days.

That is, until one young labourer, quite by accident, happened upon the entrance to an entire system of underground tunnels, after mindlessly flicking away a cigarette butt. The butt had made its way down an unseen crevice, and from there began to smoulder amongst the debris of tangled roots. Smoke could be seen rising out from the earth. Upon investigation, the men realised there was hollow space beneath.

The young man quickly ran to the site manager's office to inform him of their findings.

'Er, sorry, boss. You might want to take a look at this?' He nervously adjusted his high-vis.

'What is it?' the manager snapped.

'We've found something, boss. Dunno what it is to be

23

honest, never seen anything like it,' the workman replied.

Irritated by the unexpected interruption, the manager huffed as he stood up from his desk and begrudgingly followed the workman.

To add to his vexation, it seemed all work had ceased. Groups of burly, sour-faced men gathered in packs, cigarettes hung precariously from unshaven lips and dirt incrusted fingers. They were hovering on top of a mound of earth, perched like curious gorillas.

'What the hell is this? Why are you all just standing there? Get to work,' he shouted.

No one answered or moved, they all continued to stare down at the ground.

Before them, was the distinct outlines of an underground maze. However, they failed to notice how all the tunnels seemed to converge into one area. With all manner of tombstones and tokens of remembrance dispatched to the tip, they had no way of knowing it was the grave of Matthew Hopkins, witch finder general extraordinaire, from which the tunnels burrowed out.

It is said that after a year and a half of Hopkin's successful crusade across Essex, condemning hundreds of innocent women to death for witchcraft, the witch finder general disappeared. Some have said he himself was accused of witchcraft, and when tested or 'swam' he drowned. Others have said he succumbed to pulmonary tuberculosis. That is all the history books can tell you of his demise.

'Oh Christ,' the manager swore under his breath.

'I guess this means we need to pause construction?' the workman mused, scratching his chin.

The manager took a deep breath, tilted his head, and closed his eyes, 'We've got to report this. This is going to put our timelines right out. You may as well dismiss the men for the rest of the day.'

'Alright, I'll let them know they can go home early. What about tomorrow?' asked the workman.

'They'll be called if they're needed,' the manager muttered.

The men were sent home and were grateful to hit the pub earlier than expected. Robert Pilkins on the other hand, stood before the etched earth, and bit his lip in consternation. This was the last thing he needed.

The night quickly descended, and storms from the west were swiftly closing in, with thick clouds obscuring the iridescent moon.

The site manager ran his hand through his retreating hairline. The day had brought several unexpected pitfalls. There were no records, no surveys or reports that had hitherto identified the presence of the underground structure. Not only did it compromise what was assumed to be stable ground on which to build, it presented several issues that would delay the project indefinitely. As he continued staring at the plans, a creeping sense of dread began to dawn on him – if the authorities decided to investigate this archaeological find, it would bankrupt the company.

With a deep sigh, he reached inside his jacket for his hipflask. Taking a hearty swig, he swallowed it without a trace of feeling and refocused, deciding to look at the grounds himself, without the gormless glare of the workmen following him.

Stepping out into the chill air, he took a deep breath before descending the stairs away from his office.

He crossed the yard, which was eerily still. He paused, having thought he saw something out of the corner of his eye, scurrying along the ground. A rat most likely, he thought. He continued to the mound of earth the workmen had occupied earlier to look out over the site.

He marvelled at the intricacy of it – a hedge maze of burial earth. He realised that the formation seemed to be leading to a single point. So preoccupied with where the tunnels were leading, he failed to notice the ground beneath his feet begin to crack. Much to his surprise, his ankle slipped down a tight crevice. He cried out from pain as his ankle snapped. The ground shivered and crumbled to dust. He fell through the ground, plunging some six feet into the earth.

Coughing, choking and blinded by dust and earth, it took him a few moments for his eyes to acclimatise to the darkness that had enveloped him.

He struggled to reach for a lighter in his jeans pocket, and clumsily thumbed the friction wheel so that he might have some light to illuminate the almost impenetrable gloom. Sputtering to life, the lighter provided a small glimmer from which he was able to glean that the tunnel walls, though laced by millions of white roots, were themselves smooth and lead off in several directions.

The tunnels were tight and winding. With barely enough room to move, the site manager shuffled against the walls, which crumbled as he shifted to laying on his back. He calculated his situation – his ankle was broken, he was unable to stand, his phone was back in his office, there was no one to call for help – he was alone.

He heard a low grumbling growl, a noise of shifting earth, of roots being torn asunder. Fear washed over him in that moment.

'Wh … wh … what was that?'

He shifted against the dirt to look this way and that, but only darkness greeted him.

The noise grew louder and closer.

He desperately fumbled with the lighter for a glint of light.

A spray of dirt hit him in the face.

Something gripped his good foot.

He let out a little scream.

Frantically, he dragged himself away along the ground, feeling the walls crumbling around him as he did so, all the while the growl grew ever louder, ever closer.

He was going to be buried alive with this ... this thing.

He was sure of it.

'Please, God, no, please.' He pleaded as he scrambled through the dirt.

The tunnel walls widened and opened up, revealing a darkening sky thick with clouds. His ragged breath danced on the air. A single break in the cloud exposed a silvery beam of moonlight. To Mr Pilkins' horror, hunched before him was a creature that had the shape of a human, but in all other respects, was devoid of any perceivable humanity. Its skin hung in tatters on its blackened bones. Where its eyes should have been, were two deep wells, that oozed with indistinguishable gore. Its mouth hung agape and revealed a cavernous hole that writhed with glistening black beetles and worms.

His heart gave a painful lurch as the vision before him resumed its descent on him. Blind with terror, and clutching his chest, he frantically kicked his legs, trying to shuffle away, scrambling in the dirt, the taste and smell and touch of mud cloying his every sense, except the sense of fear.

In that final moment, he wailed like an animal mad with pain.

Fire in the Sky – By David Hawkins

'There's fire in the sky!'

My brother, Arty, never slept. He could stay awake for England, always saying that night time was more interesting than the day with its hidden mysteries and unknown shadows. He thought the best things happened at night. By best, of course, he meant scariest. Sharing a room with him was a different kind of nightmare.

'William! Wake up. You'll miss it. Wake up, you imbecile.'

Opening my eyes, taking in the darkness, I could see his outline in red, pulsing as the light fluctuated. He stared out of the window. I rolled over and out of bed and drank in the scene.

The sky was indeed on fire. Flames shaped like clouds and red darting shooting stars repeating and dashing towards the ball of flame that was slowly turning and falling.

'What is it?' I asked, sleep still sticky in my eyes.

'What is it? What is it? It's war, innit? Those are Germans and they're on fire. Quick, let's go and see where they land.'

As he spoke, Arty was pulling on his trousers, slipping

naked feet into his boots, untangling yesterday's shirt from a heap on the floor and wrestling it on. I wasn't long in copying.

Outside, we picked up our bicycles and immediately began peddling into the darkness down the Norsey Road and around the edge of the field. The falling blaze lit our journey, and we turned down Jacksons Lane. The huge round ball of fire appeared to sink and squash, and seconds later, a loud breath of noise could be heard. I could feel the heat against my face.

The field was on fire. It was Snails Hall Farm. We had crossed the field regularly on summer evenings, Arty and me. We knew it well. We knew how it dropped to the east towards Great Burstead and rose to the west as it stretched towards the high street. We didn't need to pedal as we were approaching from the west and followed the drop of the road, but we did regardless, and furiously at that. We didn't want to miss a thing.

Passing the farmhouse, a ghost figure appeared, draped in white. It was Deborah, still in her nightdress. Arty and I knew her from Sunday School, and we braked sharply. Even in the intense moment, we had time for the lovely Deborah.

'What is it?' she asked. 'I heard an engine passing my window. Thought it was a flying train! The glass was shakin'.' Her voice was a tremble.

'Look, something has crashed up in the field. It's on fire.'

'It was on fire before it crashed.' Arty pointed out. 'It was as if it were being hit by shooting stars, but it was one of our aeroplanes shooting at it.'

'What was it?'

'One of those Zeppelin things.'

'A what?'

'Those German flying machines. Must have found itself lost on the way to London,' he said before riding off into the darkness towards the bundle of flame.

I was distracted by two bicycles whizzing past, accompanied by shrill whistles. The local bobbies on bikes were charging down Jacksons Lane but Arty was some way ahead of them. He was always one step ahead of the law.

'Deborah, I'd better go follow my brother.' I lifted my left foot and pushed on the pedal, tyres crunching on loose stones.

'Be careful, William,' were her parting words.

I had to leave the bike at the edge of the field, hidden in a bramble hedge. Police officers with lanterns lurked at the field gate, their faces lit yellow, their outlines flickering orange. Knowing the farm as I did, I arced around and over the ridge, temporarily losing sight of the bonfire before it rose in front of me again like hell-fire. My steps stuttered with the intense heat. I'd lost Arty somewhere but I knew he'd be trying to get as close as he could to the burning air. I headed that way.

I found a chunk of metal. I tried to touch it but burned my fingertips. I tried again with the cuff of my overcoat, but couldn't get a meaningful grip. Besides, something more mysterious and more terrible stole my attention, a lumpen shape to my left. The detail was pronounced only by the light from the blaze still perhaps a quarter of a mile away, but it was unmistakably a man. He was still, his arms stretched out, face down, one of his legs at a crazy angle. Grabbing at his jacket's coarse material and with my other hand gripping his belt, I turned him. His eyes were wide with terror, his mouth agape as if screaming at death. Worse, his jaw was twisted awry. I turned and vomited into the grass.

Wiping my mouth, I ran forward shouting my brother's name. I didn't know fire could burn so loudly. The night was lit up now that I was close, a macabre red as if the air itself were blood. Again, I shouted my brother's name. A caped, bat-like figure appeared.

31

'Move away lad, it's not safe.'

'My brother's here somewhere.'

'It's not safe. Fire spreads,' the policeman repeated. He came close and shoved me backwards. 'Move away. I'll not tell you again.'

There was a crowd now, twenty or more people gathered in nightclothes overladen with dark overcoats. Their faces reflected reds and oranges as the flames danced in the air.

Moving on, shouting my brother's name, I circled the scene. The length of it was enormous; it took me more than a minute to traverse from one end to the other and round to the other side. Then I saw him, a silhouette against flame, arms out as if absorbing heat, crucified against the flame.

'Arty! Arty!'

I ran towards him. Only when I reached his side did he notice me. He turned, smiled – a grimace really – and he dropped his arms to his side. His face carried a rich expression.

'I saw him, William, with my own eyes. I saw him go!'

Looking about, I saw nobody. I could only detect Arty and the dark space between us and around us, plus, the boom of burning wreckage and the savage air.

'Saw what? What are you talking about?'

It was then I noticed the body at his feet. This one was face up, eyes wide, a shape of a scream where his mouth should be.

'I saw his soul. I saw him die, Will, and I saw his soul leave him. Like a small, black bird. It flew up into the sky and the gates of heaven opened and took him in. And then he was still. It was beautiful, William. I was with him and saw him leave.'

Looking down at the empty body and then at the stretching sky, I imagined I saw it too – a soul leaving a body and flying away to find its own peace.

A Beast of a Storm – By Lisa Horner

Canvey Island. 31 January 1953.

'Steady on girl!' John said, as Shirley jolted forward after a powerful gust of wind had nearly lifted her off the pavement. He put his arm around her protectively. It was a bracing Saturday evening. A full moon highlighted the frosty, glistening pavements. John was escorting Shirley back home after one of their monthly evenings of games and entertainment hosted by his mum and dad. At the end of the evening, it was the tradition for Dad to play the piano while they all enjoyed a sing-song.

They soon arrived at her prefabricated bungalow.

'What a night!' John exclaimed. 'I think there might be a bad storm!'

'I think you're right John, I can't wait to get in the warm!'

She quickly kissed him on the cheek and thanked him for a great night. John smiled and returned her kiss.

On the way home, John wrapped his coat tightly around him as he struggled to walk against the wind. Shivering, he let himself in and raced upstairs to get himself warm under the bedcovers.

A thunderous banging on the front door woke the whole house up the next morning, and John could clearly hear a siren going off in the distance. He leapt down the stairs, two steps at a time, and opened the porch door, pulling the front door closed behind him because of the high winds. Councillor Ron Watts was standing there looking extremely serious. While he was clinging onto the door frame to keep upright, his comb-over was blown to stand up on end, revealing his shiny, balding pate. John caught his balance while a gust of air smelling of sewage and sea salt blasted him in the face.

'The sea wall has broken,' the councillor shouted. 'The water is around eight feet high down there! We need men to help us rescue people who are still in their houses. Can you and your brothers help man some boats?'

'Yes! I'll get Syd and Jack!' John yelled back.

John went back in and found his whole family standing there, looking horrified. Mum hugged her three sons tearfully and told them to be careful. They got dressed in no time and joined the councillor and a growing group of men. John, Syd and Jack passed disbelieving looks between themselves as they witnessed the flooded landscape. Syd and John got an old Coast Guard's boat and Jack and his friend got another.

A little disorientated, not knowing which way to go, they rowed through household contents and debris. Following this, they rowed past a dead pig and a cow. Syd choked back some tears, making John swing around to see what he was looking at: a dog floating lifelessly on the murky waves. It could have been their dog, Skipper, if they lived nearer the estuary. Getting nearer to the sea wall, the green-grey water was lapping just below the top floor windows of the two-storey houses. The bungalows were just showing their rooftops.

'Oh no!' shouted John, as it occurred to him that Shirley lived in a bungalow. 'We've got to get to Shirley's bungalow!'

'God, yes! Let's head in that direction,' said Syd.

Suddenly an enormous wave thrust the boat forward. The lads held on tightly as the boat rocked from side to side. They felt the boat lightly shake as a local cat jumped down from the branches of a tree.

'Hold on tight moggy,' said Syd.

They spotted Shirley, who looked so small, sitting on her roof. Nearby, a man, a woman and two small girls were sitting on their bungalow roof. As they got nearer Shirley saw them and it became apparent that her parents weren't with her. The lads rowed very close to the building and Shirley jumped into the boat, then they went to get the family. The man offered to take over John's oar so that he could comfort Shirley who was crying uncontrollably. She calmed herself enough to explain what had happened.

'I woke up as the water started to soak my bed covers. I went to Mum and Dad's room and I ... I couldn't wake them. They had drowned in their sleep!' Shirley's face sunk into John's chest. Then she took a deep breath and continued. 'I tried to move them up and away from the water but I couldn't, I just had to leave them there!'

Then the little girls started to cry. The ginger cat made its way to them and knew instinctively to give them some comfort. It purred its hypnotic purr and this calmed the girls who stroked and cuddled the cat; their sobbing gradually subsiding.

The sound of motors running made John look up. They were near land, and could see soldiers escorting people onto lorries. In the distance they could see more soldiers building a barricade on the sea wall with sandbags. The tides ripped against the sea wall, soaking the men.

The family got onto the lorry with their newly adopted pet. John stood with Shirley and held her tightly, trying to calm her down before she had to leave.

'I will find you sweetheart,' he whispered, then kissed her tenderly on the lips. Fresh tears rolled down Shirley's cheeks but a tiny piece of hope gleamed in her eyes.

As the lorry left, John and Syd were glad to see their brother and his friend. Jack noticed his brothers' distraught faces and asked them what was wrong. They were all terribly saddened by the news about Shirley's parents. Jack told them that they had rescued some people who were in an awful state, they were suffering from hypothermia and they had to get them onto an ambulance and off to Southend hospital. They'd been on their roof, freezing for several hours.

3 February 1953.

John, Syd, Jack and their father, Fred, had been doing all they could in the rescue effort. Their mother, Daisy, had been helping over in Benfleet in one of the rescue centres making sure that people were clothed warmly, fed and looked after. Even though their home wasn't drastically affected by the sea, John's family had to move out as the whole area had become unsanitary. Daisy's sister, Ivy, had invited them all to stay with them in Benfleet.

Daisy had some important news to share.

'The Queen Mother and Princess Margaret are coming down to the centre this afternoon. You've got to come down boys, and you Fred. You've all worked so hard, you need a rest!'

They didn't need a lot of persuading. When they arrived the rest of the family were humbled by the sight they saw.

Here and there mattresses were occupied by people laying in depressed states, and in shock as their whole worlds had been devastated in a matter of hours.

John looked around sorrowfully. Then, walking through the main doors, he recognised the family that he and Syd had rescued. He nudged Syd and they both walked up to them, utterly delighted to see them faring so well. Behind them walked Shirley. She saw John and ran up to him, he took her in his arms.

'I've been staying with Jessie and Mike, we were lucky! We've been put up in an unoccupied house near here, and I've really got fond of these girls,' said Shirley, smiling.

'I've been thinking about you constantly, every day, and wondering how you are.' John looked at Shirley intensely, drinking her in. *She seems to get prettier every day* he thought.

'Me too,' said Shirley, her face becoming serious, 'and worrying about you! Praying that you'd be safe.' Then she looked up into his eyes and said, 'How can I ever thank you for rescuing me!'

John moved his head towards her and they started kissing, it felt natural, and all the turbulence and upheaval of the last few days resulted in a passionate, emotional embrace.

'Put her down!' laughed Jack.

The pair moved apart just as Councillor Ron Watts entered the hall. He announced, 'Ladies and gentlemen, if you would all get ready for the Queen Mother and Princess Margaret.'

As the royal pair entered the hall, the councillor bowed and, as they walked through, men and women started to bow and curtsy.

'Really, there is no need for all this protocol. Please relax,' exclaimed the Queen Mother.

The Queen Mother and Princess Margaret wanted to hear everyone's story. They proved to be sympathetic listeners and gave words of comfort where needed as they passed through the crowd of devastated people. Shirley told them how the brothers had rescued people and that she was rescued by John and Syd. The lads were all thanked for their efforts and called heroes. The little girls told Princess Margaret that they now had a new cat but missed their dog who still hadn't been found. The Queen Mother sympathised with Shirley when she told her of the harrowing loss of her parents. She put her hand lightly on Shirley's shoulder.

'I'm so absolutely sorry for your terrible loss my dear girl,' said the grand lady.

After the royal visit John invited Shirley to his aunt's house. Daisy took the opportunity to talk to her.

'I knew your parents for many years and I owe it to them to ask you if you would like to stay with us? For as long as you like. That is, when we can move back in.'

John put his arm around Shirley's waist and smiled.

'Thanks Mum, do you know that Shirley and I are courting? Will that change anything?'

'That's fine, we'll figure out some sort of arrangement.'

'Thank you, Daisy, I really, really appreciate that!' said Shirley. 'It makes all this a little less terrible!'

That evening they all huddled around the black and white television. The presenter explained in his cut glass accent that on 31 January Scotland was struck first. At Costa Hill in the Orkney Islands a wind speed of one hundred and twenty-six miles per hour was recorded. The force of the sea and extremely high winds snapped telephone and electricity cables, making communication impossible. The storm had made its way around the east coast and had hit Norfolk, Suffolk and the eastern parts of Essex before it had got to Canvey. It also reached Belgium and had a particularly devastating effect on the Netherlands. Everybody gasped when they found out that fifty people had died in Canvey and there were still a few people in hospital in a critical state. Thousands of homes on the island had been destroyed and there were over twenty thousand seriously damaged homes in the United Kingdom.

As the presenter continued, Shirley's mind drifted back to the early hours of 1 February when she had discovered her lifeless parents. John held her while she sobbed helplessly against his broad chest. She felt so frail but John's embrace strengthened her and he vowed he would always protect her, if she'd let him.

It was such hideous news to take in that everybody sat looking down, mournfully. John wanted to lift Shirley's mood and there was something he was desperate to ask. So, he got down on one knee.

'Dear, sweet Shirley, my love for you has been growing as big as that beast of a storm! Please do me the honour of being my wife?'

Shirley replied, trembling with emotion. 'My world broke apart in the early hours of that morning, but your love and friendship gave me hope. I would be honoured to be your wife John, and to be part of this lovely family. Let's take it one step at a time though, after all it was only four days ago that I was living with my parents, oblivious to what was around the corner.'

The pair embraced and the family cheered heartily, aware that love can be found in the bleakest of times.

The Last Straw – By Janet Howson

Matilda wiped her hands on her tunic and then removed her wimple. She was hot and light- headed through hunger. Smoke from the firepit in the middle of the small living space made her cough. The heat was needed, though. The wattle and daub walls didn't keep out the piercing cold, especially at night as she lay on her mattress stuffed with hay that made her itch.

She had been up since break of day, bringing in crops. Now she was home, her job was to clean their cruck house and try to get rid of the bugs and filth. Their cow, precious for her nutritious milk, lived with them and Matilda had to deal with the cow's excrement. Matilda was a sensitive girl, and she was aware of the unhygienic conditions she lived in. She was allowed one bath a year, sometimes two. She knew it wasn't healthy to have any more than this. She was fourteen, the same age as the teenage king, Richard the Second. She was aware of the unpopularity of this young Royal. She was lucky. Her uncle, Jack Straw, who she lived with, had taught her to read and write. He explained how only a very few people in England could read. He had been born an unfree peasant but had chosen ordination to become a priest; one of the few lawful ways to escape serfdom. He told Matilda this meant he couldn't take a wife and lie with her. He was educated though and passed on his learning to Matilda, his only family. Her father, Jack's brother, had died of The Black Death and her mother had died soon after in childbirth. The boy was buried with her, the boy her father had always hoped for.

Matilda moved to the table. On it was a pile of turnips, onions, cabbages, and leeks. Her uncle had managed to get a small piece of beef for Matilda to make a potage. She would add rice and barley to thicken the vegetable juices and herbs to flavour it. She was a good cook, but they rarely had meat, relying more on nuts and grain. Existence was hard. Jack said The Black Death had taken its toll, leaving a shortage of labour that meant less production, so the landowners' profits were eroded by a disintegration of trading. Matilda had heard that it killed half the population of England. The Hundred Years War had resulted in high taxation followed by the unpopular Poll Taxes, three in the last four years.

A shout made Matilda drop her knife. She stooped to pick it up. Then there was a scream and the sound of men running. The mayhem continued, male voices arguing and taunting. She thought she recognised Jack's voice. She knew he had gone out before daybreak for a meeting in the churchyard of St Mary's Church in Great Baddow. He had told her it was about the crippling taxation the serfs were forced to pay. He must have already returned to Brentwood. She left everything and ran outside, trying to work out where the noise was coming from. Suddenly she saw them. Her uncle was leading a group of men armed with spiked clubs, axes, flails, and pitchforks. They were chanting and Matilda could make out some of the words.

'All men should be free and equal!' 'Stop the Poll Tax!' 'Share the wealth!'

They stamped on the ground or used their weapons to form a rhythm. It was threatening and grew more so as their numbers increased with men from the town joining in. Some of them were men Matilda knew. She had grown up with their children, playing and laughing together in the fields and woods. They were kind men, not like these men she saw before her. What had happened to make them like this?

She knew her uncle had been discontented and angry for a long time. He would meet his friends and neighbours in the local Inns, heads bowed over sheets of paper, huddled together in case they were heard and reported to the authorities. When he came back to their cramped home, he was moody and silent, pacing about in the small space, hands behind his back, a frown creasing his forehead. He wouldn't talk to Matilda about it and when she begged him to sit down and tell her what the matter was, he said she was too young to be worrying about such matters. However, he didn't know she had overheard the gossip in the market place, all about the unfair taxes and how hard it was for the men and their families to survive. She knew that was why he was so unhappy.

She tried to run over to her uncle who by now was shouting at an important looking man in good clothes and leather boots but was pushed roughly out of the way by an official. She heard her uncle call the man's name, 'You're an arse John Brampton, take your sniffling snails and get out of our town, we will not be paying your Poll Tax, not now or ever.'

The man, John Brampton, called over to his companions to help. 'Come. Let's get rid of these lawless vermin.' A group of young men joined him and started pushing her uncle around; he retaliated and they hit him. That was the final trigger. Men appeared from nowhere to support her uncle, hordes of them eager to atone for the wrong doings heaped

43

on them. They fought without fear. Those without weapons used their fists and feet. The shouting was unbearable and frightening, so Matilda hid between two buildings and watched the battle. The officials had no chance against the unbridled discontent that poured out of the serfs. Matilda heard a deathly cry followed by another and another. She prayed no one had been killed. She had heard that sound before as neighbour had turned on neighbour in disputes of land and goods.

One minute the street was filled with desperate men, the next it was practically empty, like a ghost town. Matilda slowly emerged from her hiding place. There were three bodies on the floor, three of the tax collectors. The man, John Brampton, had escaped. She looked round for her uncle; he was nowhere to be seen. She ran down the street calling his name, banging open the door of the pub he favoured but he wasn't there. Had they taken him to London to face being thrown in the Tower? She had heard terrible tales of torture, starvation and execution. How rebels and traitors were drawn, hanged and quartered. The image filled her with fear and she tasted vomit in her mouth.

Then she saw him, leading a group of men carrying heaps of books and papers. They strode to the centre of the town throwing their loads down and forming a circle round them. Then a flame appeared brought by the baker who always kept his embers going in his ovens. He lit the papers and they flared up bright and dancing, consuming the books and papers easily. The men stamped and clapped their hands and her uncle led the chanting again.

'Abolish serfdom!' 'Reduce the taxes!' 'Out with the king's officials.'

They continued until the flames subsided. A few of the stronger men dragged the tax collector's bodies away, the others trailed off back to their homes. Many were pulled out by their wives and children, worried that they could be arrested. Her uncle though, had no wife, so it was up to Matilda to look after him. She ran to him and he took her in his arms and hugged her tightly.

'We got rid of them, Matty, those swine who would rob us blind. We've even burnt all the court records of the town and ledgers to do with the taxation. It won't stop at this neither, Watt Tyler is leading his men from Kent to London to protest and the men from Essex will be with them.' Matilda had never seen her uncle so happy. He pulled his strong shoulders back and smiled to himself. 'If those stuck-up pigs in London think they can walk all over us countrymen they are sadly mistaken.' He gave Matilda a hug, 'We Straws are a tough breed. Now come on girl lets return to our home together and have that potage.'

So, Matilda and Jack ate and laughed as they enjoyed their food, unaware that the scene they had both just witnessed was to lead to a revolt against the government and laws of the country by serfs and others who had been so tested to the end of all patience with the crippling demands on their purses. This would be known as The Peasants Revolt and it would be a significant episode in English History, influencing future decisions that were made on taxation.

Five hundred and sixty-five years later, a John Whitaker Straw was born in Buckhurst Hill, Essex. His father was an insurance clerk and a former industrial chemist. His mother was a teacher at the independent Oaklands School. He later changed his name to Jack in honour of the original Jack Straw. He was educated at Oaklands then Brentwood School. He went on to gain a law degree at the University of Leeds and became a barrister. He succeeded Barbara Castle as Labour MP for Blackburn in 1979 and served in parliament under

Tony Blair in various cabinet positions: Secretary of State, Leader of the House of Commons, Secretary of State for Foreign and Commonwealth Affairs and Home Secretary.

In 1997 as Home Secretary, Straw ordered a public enquiry into the Matters Arising from the Death of Steven Lawrence. The report concluded the Police Force was 'institutionally racist.' Straw commented that ordering the enquiry was 'The single most important decision I made as Home Secretary.'

Whilst Jack Straw was in the Labour Shadow Cabinet, Margaret Thatcher, Conservative Prime Minister, introduced a Community Charge, commonly known as the Poll Tax. This was seen to be grossly unfair to the less well-off and was opposed by the Labour Party. This resulted in mass protests, demonstrations, riots and refusal to pay. This was similar to the original Poll Tax and like it was abolished. History repeating itself.

So, had the genes passed on down from Jack and his daughter Matilda, through all those generations? It would be satisfying to think so. However, we can say the original Jack was definitely not 'The Last Straw'.

Return to Plotlands – By Dawn Knox

2016

You wouldn't normally expect to find a sleeping baby on the luggage rack of a train. Today, there'd probably be outrage and blunt comments about health and safety, but in 1930, when the world was more relaxed about such things, it happened at least once – or so I'm told. The baby girl in question was me, although being fast asleep, I remember nothing about my first railway journey.

As the train rocked from side to side on its way from Fenchurch Street Station in London to the Essex countryside, my elder sister, Hannah, was wedged between our parents and their luggage. Years later, she told me of her envy at my elevated position, high above the other passengers' heads. At six years of age, she was too heavy for Mum to carry for long, and her initial excitement at travelling soon turned to boredom when she found her view restricted to legs, suitcases, and boxes.

And worse, once we'd arrived at Laindon railway station, there had been a long walk through the countryside, along muddy, rutted roads. Footsore and weary, she'd burst into tears on arrival at our destination.

Apparently, Mum had cried too.

It would be many years before it occurred to me how disappointed Mum would have been, at discovering the "country chalet" Dad had inherited from his uncle, was more reminiscent of a garden shed, than of the picturesque, thatched cottage of which she'd dreamed.

By the time I was old enough to form memories of my own, Dad's inherited chalet had ceased to be our weekend retreat in the country and was our full-time residence.

No longer a small, wooden shack, it was now a brick-built bungalow, called Swallowmere, with a wooden veranda at the front, and neat garden and vegetable plot at the back.

Dad, Hannah and I loved it, and if Mum secretly longed to return to the rented, two-up, two-down terraced house we'd vacated in Stepney, she didn't show it. Or perhaps she did, but I was too wrapped up in my own young life to notice.

On the days Hannah and I weren't at school, we'd meet up with friends after breakfast, and wander for miles until the sun began to dip. We took chunks of bread on our expeditions, or if the apples were ripe on the tree in the garden, we'd pick a few and stuff them in our pockets to keep us going.

Be home before dark. That was the only rule and rather than risk Mum's wrath, we tried our best to keep to that. Often arriving back at Swallowmere so out of breath, we couldn't gulp air into our lungs fast enough. Mud-splattered, thorn-scratched and in the autumn – blackberry-stained.

'Those girls are becoming feral, Tom,' Mum would complain to Dad, although she never stopped us from going out. I often marvel at our lack of sensitivity – selfishly eager to play, without giving a second's thought to all the tasks Mum would have to perform every day. Fetching water from a standpipe some way from our house, cooking on an ancient oil stove, feeding the chickens, tending the vegetables, keeping our home free from the omnipresent mud and performing the multitude of other tasks we scarcely noticed.

Mum's fears we were running wild were unfounded. Yes, we wandered over fields and through woods, but we had our own unspoken code of conduct. The older ones often moaned about their younger, slower siblings, but we all played together and looked out for each other. The Plotland community was so closely knit that nothing could be hidden from all those adult eyes. Any bad behaviour would have resulted in trouble with your own parents and everyone else's parents, too.

Sometimes, Mum would insist Hannah and I helped with the chores, although if given a choice, we always opted for the jobs that allowed us to roam. We were more than happy to go to the small general store near the Lower Dunton Road to buy paraffin oil for the cooker because Dad usually slipped us a ha'penny or two to spend on sweets. And when we went to the dairy, the farmer's wife would always give us a mug of frothy, fresh milk to drink before we carried our overflowing jugs back to Mum. Stomachs gurgling and the smell of cream in our nostrils from the yellow milk 'moustaches' on our upper lips.

However, the times I remember most vividly were when we were sent to the Colony to buy vegetables or fruit.

Before our first visit, I'd told Hannah I didn't want to go with her because I was afraid of bees.

She'd laughed. 'It's not a bee colony, you idiot. It's a place where paupers do things.'

'What sort of things?'

'Oh, grow stuff ... and do other things,' she'd said vaguely.

I'd tagged along with her and her friends. I had no idea

49

what to expect and was surprised to see a lot of men working in a field.

'So, what is a pauper?' I'd asked loudly, still not convinced there wouldn't be a swarm of bees.

'Shh!' she'd replied sharply, elbowing me in the ribs. Red-faced with embarrassment, her friends rushed ahead to the general store, leaving us behind.

'Honestly! You're so ignorant,' Hannah had added, rolling her eyes to the skies.

Mum later explained that while there may indeed be beehives in the Colony, it was actually an experimental farming community. It had been set up for paupers – or poor men – many of whom were old soldiers, who'd otherwise have been forced to live in the Poplar Workhouse in London.

'A kind man bought the farm and gave it to the guardians in charge of the workhouse, and any of the poor men fit enough to work on the land were sent from Poplar to Dunton.'

It had been a surprise to learn workhouse guardians might move men to different parts of the country just because they didn't have much money. I desperately hoped no one had overheard my innocent, but tactless, question and thought I'd been poking fun at them.

On each trip into the Colony after that, I'd quietly observed the men who worked in the orchard and gardens. Of course, I was aware it was rude to stare, but I was so fascinated, I lingered on the way to the general store and then on my way home. It wasn't until I'd grown up, I realised what a truly remarkable place it had been. A self-contained village with dormitory accommodation and workshops of all kinds: cobblers, tailors, carpenters, plumbers … And so many farm buildings like the slaughterhouse, dairy, stables, cowsheds …

I also realised there was very little difference between the men of the Colony and many of our elderly neighbours in

Plotlands. It was just a question of finance. There, but for the grace of God ...

Not that any of the Plotland families would have considered themselves rich – with the possible exception of the man who built his bungalow out of Italian marble. But nobody went without.

When one family was in need, the others rallied around, offering help or gifts of food. We were pioneering East Enders, and we'd brought with us a strong sense of community. It didn't matter what unfamiliar problems the Essex countryside threw at us; we rose to the challenge for ourselves and our neighbours.

Of course, occasional arguments broke out, but they were usually resolved before Saturday night when many of the families got together for a party. On the rare weekend when there were no birthdays or anniversaries, a reason could always be found to celebrate.

During the summer, we'd get together around a bonfire in someone's garden or if it rained, the men would put up canvas awnings under which they'd arrange trestle tables and a variety of deckchairs and stools. Each family would bring plates of food and homemade beer that we youngsters tried our best to sample.

As the drink flowed, the adults became less vigilant, and our attempts were more successful. It was dreadful stuff – bitter and pungent. But after a while, we got used to the taste.

We roasted chestnuts on a shovel in the fire, and later, there'd be singing and dancing to a wind-up gramophone, unless Mr. Jefferson could be persuaded to play his fiddle.

And then, abruptly, my carefree life on Plotlands came to an end. It was 1939 and the outbreak of war marked the end of my sunny childhood. The first time I saw German bombers fly overhead on their way to devastate London, I wondered if the world would ever be the same again. And for me, it never was.

We became familiar with gas masks, ration books, blackout, bombing raids ... For the following six years, the life that had once been so simple was now edged with anxiety and dread.

Trips to London to visit our family ceased, and our house filled with a succession of relatives who came to stay. Some remained, but others were evacuated to more rural areas, and as the years passed, older cousins left to join up – some never to return.

After the beginning of the war, the Colony closed. I've no idea where all the men went – perhaps back to Poplar. The area was turned into a hospital ready for bomb victims, although I don't think it was ever used. Then later, the army took it over and stationed troops there. You should've seen the tents in the fields and orchard – it was quite a sight.

Then, they left, and I think the RAF took it over, but once the war had ended, I don't know what happened to the farm.

After the war, I expected everyone to move back – for people to pick up where they'd left off, but Plotlands was never the same again. Many people never returned, and bungalows fell into disrepair. Then I met my Robert and after we'd married, we moved away to the south coast.

And now, in 2016, at the age of 86, I have returned. I stand here, near the site of Swallowmere, and I survey what was once my home, searching for something familiar.

I recognise nothing.

Not that there's anything wrong with my memory. But there are no points of reference. The neat bungalows, wooden shacks and even the train carriage that served as a home are all gone. The gates and the fences that marked each property are no more, and nature has reclaimed the land. The undergrowth has repossessed our carefully tended vegetable plot and swallowed the foundations of Swallowmere; creeping to the foot of the apple tree that grows in what had once been our front garden. In its time, that tree had been a space rocket, a car and a ship. We hid in its canopy, we swung from its branches, and we gorged ourselves on its sweet fruit, and now it has turned feral, just like Mum feared Hannah and I had all those years ago.

I close my eyes and imagine the avenue once again lined with diverse and distinct homes, mothers hanging out washing, fathers whistling as they worked in the garden. The smell of the grass, freshly cut with a scythe. I can almost see children strolling towards me with fishing nets and jam jars, calling for the young ones to stop dawdling.

Where is everyone now? Tears prick my eyes at the thought that so many of those people I once knew are no longer with us. And I yearn to experience that long-ago peace.

Sadly, I turn and walk away. It's unlikely I'll ever return. And I say a final, silent farewell to everyone I knew. Then, it occurs to me I'm not leaving them behind at all. In fact, I'm taking them with me. Every single person I once knew is safely held in my heart.

Humpty Dumpty Sat on a Wall
– By G K Lomax

Colchester, July 1648

The sound of riders approaching made young Sam Tanner raise his head. 'Now what have we here?' he asked.

Heads turned. There were two riders, one a man of high rank to judge by his dress. With a start, John Caldwell recognised him and urged his fellows to their feet. The men, who'd been lounging in the shade afforded by St Mary's church, which had been incorporated into the town walls left by the Romans, reluctantly obeyed, with the exception of one man, who had his hat over his face and was snoring gently.

'That includes you, George Simpson,' Caldwell said, prodding the sleeping man none too gently with his foot. 'That's Sir Charles.'

Simpson, the oldest soldier of the group, had the ability to make himself comfortable anywhere and to fall asleep at will. He woke up, raised his hat a few inches, took in the scene, then lowered his hat again. He was soon snoring once more.

Lieutenant General Sir Charles Lucas ignored him and his companions. He rode up to St Mary's and looked up at the tower.

'There you are, Thompson,' he said to his companion, 'tall enough to give you the extra range you need, wouldn't you say? Flat roof, I'm told, so it should serve.'

Thompson was a gaunt man in his fifties, with a battle-hardened air about him. He had thin straggly hair, three days' worth of stubble and a patch over his left eye. He scratched his chin thoughtfully. 'Aye, Sir Charles, what you suggest may be possible. But once up there, she'll draw fire from every gun Fairfax has.'

'Which is why I've ordered our guns to concentrate here. They may outnumber us in cavalry, but we've more guns than them – and bigger ones, too. I doubt they have anything capable of firing balls over six pounds, and they'll just bounce off these stones.' He patted the tower affectionately. 'The churches of England are built strong. Fairfax can fire every piece he has, but it won't do him any good. I'm sure he's sent for siege guns, but it'll be weeks before they get here. An artillery duel; short and brutal. Smash their guns, blast a hole in their ranks, then sally forth and put them to flight. What do you think?'

Simpson stopped snoring. 'A six-pound ball may bounce off a church tower,' he said from under his hat, 'but it can make a fair mess of you and me.'

Tanner, who was accustomed to Simpson's ability to hear in his sleep, looked anxiously at Lucas, but he didn't seem to have heard. Instead, he and Thompson turned and rode slowly away.

'What do you suppose that was about?' Tanner asked.

'It means work for someone,' Caldwell said, 'and by someone, I mean us.'

The next day, two wagons loaded with timber and rope appeared. Men sweated as they carried baulks of timber up to the roof of St Mary's tower. There, a scaffold was erected. Its purpose was clear: one or more pieces were to be sited on top of the tower, the better to bombard the besiegers. Several guns were brought up as the day wore on – the usual mixture of cannon, culverins, and sakers – but none were hauled up. When work stopped for supper bets were taken on which guns would be chosen.

'None of them,' said Simpson, who'd persistently managed to avoid catching an officer's eye when the heaviest work was to be done. 'At least, none that have been brought up so far.'

'What makes you so sure?' Tanner asked.

'The scaffold. It's too solid for any of the guns here. One-eyed Thompson wouldn't waste the timber unless he was planning on hauling a really big piece up there.'

'One-eyed Thompson?' Tanner asked.

'You saw the patch, didn't you? He lost an eye at the siege of Maastricht, back in thirty-two or thirty-three. I was there. Thompson knows his business. The real work comes tomorrow.'

'When you won't be around?' Caldwell asked.

Simpson ignored him.

'Will General Lucas' plan work?' Tanner asked. 'Blast a hole in the enemy lines and sweep them away?'

'You'd better hope so. If not, we're in for a long siege, and long sieges mean short commons. We'll be eating rats in a month – if we're lucky.'

'It won't come to that, will it?' Tanner asked. 'They'll negotiate a surrender. It's happened before.'

'It has, but don't count on it this time. Lucas has already surrendered three times in these wars. The last time he was released on account of him swearing an oath not to take up arms against Parliament again. Which oath he's broken. If he's captured a fourth time, he'll be hanged – and he knows it. No surrender for him, so empty bellies for us.'

'Unless his plan works,' Tanner said, but Simpson was already snoring.

The big gun arrived the next day. Short, squat and massive, it took a dozen horses to drag it painfully up to St Mary's. John Caldwell whistled when he saw it. 'I've never seen anything like it,' he said. 'It's huge!'

'I told you, didn't I?' Simpson told him. 'It's a mortar. Useful at sieges, but the devil's own job to cart around the country. Or to the top of a tower.'

'Why does Sir Charles want it up there?' Caldwell asked, looking up dubiously.

'Like he said to Thompson, to increase its range. Got to be able to reach Parliament's lines.'

'We're going to need every man and more when it comes time to heave it up,' Caldwell said. He looked meaningfully at Simpson, who smiled thinly.

Sam Tanner, meanwhile, had been staring awestruck at the great gun. 'It reminds me of my Uncle Humphrey,' he said suddenly.

'You uncle's a mortar?' Simpson asked him.

'No, but he's short and fat. Like a barrel on legs. Ma calls him Humpty Dumpty.'

By dint of gathering every man he could find (including a reluctant Simpson) to haul on the ropes, One-eyed Thompson succeeded in raising the newly christened Humpty Dumpty to the roof of St Mary's tower. The ropes creaked ominously, and the scaffold seemed about to collapse at one point, but the job was done. Afterwards, barrel upon barrel of gunpowder was hauled up, along with the great shot that would be fired at the enemy. Each weighed more than a hundredweight and was – as Simpson explained – a hollow iron ball filled with gunpowder, with a short fuse that was lit just before the gun was fired.

'If it lands in the right place, it can be devastating,' Simpson said, before adding, somewhat gloomily, that getting the ball to land in the right place happened maybe once every six shots, and that even then the fuse was prone to fail.

'Still,' he said, 'it'll give them something to think about.'

The bombardment began the next morning. Lucas had gathered about two dozen guns which, sheltered behind the wall, began to hammer at the besiegers. Except that hammer wasn't quite the right word. The Parliamentary troops might've been vulnerable had they been massed for an assault, but spread out as they were, balls mostly passed through their lines, doing little damage. One wagon had a wheel smashed, and a few horses were panicked, but that was about all.

Lucas, watching keenly through his glass, seemed childishly excited, however. He hopped from foot to foot, cheering each shot.

Then, with a great roar, Humpty Dumpty spoke. An awed silence fell. 'God's teeth,' Sam Tanner said, 'I felt the ground shake from down here.'

'Watch the ball, lad,' Simpson told him, 'watch the ball.'

The great iron ball was plainly visible as it rose impossibly high. For a moment it seemed to hang motionless in the clear blue sky, then it began to descend – almost vertically, Tanner thought – faster and faster until, with a thud that those watching fancied they could feel from a quarter of a mile away, it fell to earth among a cluster of Royalist tents.

There was an agonizing pause, then a titanic explosion as the shell burst asunder. Canvas flew like scraps of paper in the wind; a tree was all but shredded; men died.

The Royalists cheered, Lucas positively capered, and even old Simpson smiled. 'Half a day of this,' Lucas exclaimed, 'and we'll sweep them away as easily as a beldame shoos away a cat.'

Half a day passed. Humpty Dumpty fired eleven times, the procedure to load and prime the great mortar being frustratingly slow. Three times the shell failed to explode. Another four fell short or flew too far, causing little inconvenience to the Parliamentarians.

Lucas stopped capering. The other guns slackened their fire. One-eyed Thompson moved from gun to gun. The expression on his face didn't inspire confidence.

Suddenly, Simpson pointed. 'Look there.'

Men looked. The Parliamentarians were bringing up guns to reply. Big guns. 'If they can't fire more than a six-pound ball,' Simpson said, 'my mother's the Virgin Mary. Weeks away, my foot.'

The counter-bombardment began at five o'clock. It was directed by someone who knew his business as well as One-eyed Thompson – or better. After a few ranging shots, balls began to slam into the wall. Splinters flew; men screamed. A ball struck a culverin square on the barrel, sending it spinning and turning three men to pulp.

Lucas exhorted his men to greater efforts. 'Smash their guns,' he yelled. 'Smash them!'

A ball struck St Mary's tower. A shower of fragments fell. One-eyed Thompson climbed up to direct Humpty Dumpty's next shot.

More balls hit the stonework that Lucas had declared to be so strong; two, three. To Sam Tanner, watching in fascinated horror, it seemed that the tower trembled.

Humpty Dumpty roared again. This time the shell flew true. One of the Parliamentary guns was blasted into the air. Men cheered, but Sam Tanner did not. He'd noticed that the shock of Humpty Dumpty's last round had caused a crack to appear near the top of the tower. He shouted a warning, but no-one heard him over the sound of the guns.

Another hit on the tower. More fragments fell. Daylight could be seen where there'd been stone before.

A final hit. The top of St Mary's tower tilted, paused, began to come apart. There were cries of alarm. Then the top ten feet of the tower collapsed. A rain of stone, then shocked silence. At the foot of the tower was a heap of rubble. On top of the heap, the body of One-eyed Thompson. On top of him, on its side and with a thin coil of smoke rising from its gaping mouth, lay Humpty Dumpty.

Humpty Dumpty sat on a wall.
Humpty Dumpty had a great fall.
All the King's horses and all the King's men
Couldn't put Humpty together again.

The Parliamentarians carried the section of wall by St Mary's the next day. Abandoning their guns, the Royalists retreated into the town, where they held out for a further six weeks. They ate their rations. They ate their horses. They ate rats. The townsfolk starved and died.

When news of Cromwell's victory at Preston reached the town, the Royalists surrendered. Most of the defenders limped away to an uncertain fate. Lucas was detained. To his surprise, he wasn't hanged. He was put in front of a firing-squad instead.

Historical note

The siege of Colchester lasted from 2nd July to 28th August, with the bastion by St Mary's falling on 14th July. The tower of St Mary's was indeed partially destroyed. It was later repaired – in brick rather than stone, meaning that the extent of the damage is visible today. A man called One-eyed Thompson is said to have been among the casualties.

And was there really a gun called Humpty Dumpty? Historians are doubtful, but writers don't have to listen to them.

Cruise – By Emma Marks

Blue-white smoke poured from the spinning, shrieking rear tyres. The powerful car squirmed violently under the conflicting messages from its accelerator and brakes. The back end of the car disappeared from view. The cloud blew on toward the assembled faces that cheered the driver. Their noses filled with the smell of burning rubber and hot engine.

The car was a mostly red Ford Capri, the Mark III to be accurate, and if you want to be really precise, a 3 litre V6 Sport. It had come on a long journey from its original factory specification when it was new in 1980. Starting with wheels, the black Revolution alloys were shod with the widest, low-profile tyres that could be squeezed into the wheel arches. Those same wheel arches had been flared wider by the addition of a X-Pack, a post-production kit of fibre glass designed to replace the original wings and quarter panels, making them more bulbous in appearance. The car had lowered suspension, and it squatted with a menacing presence close to the ground, its twin headlights lasering a path through the growing dusk and tyre smoke.

In addition to the X-Pack, the obligatory large spoiler

adorned the rear part of the sloping coupe boot lid. In the 1980s, a great deal of profit was made from the idea that such spoilers aided road holding capabilities. All the X-Pack additional panels had to be riveted to the car and then painstakingly filled and sanded to blend. Due to the high cost of a professional bodyshop doing this work, money was saved, for the final glorious paint respray moment, by the car owner doing much of the preparation themselves. Cars often spent many months in this state of patchwork finery. However, this provided a talking point and, as they were mechanically fine, these cars would still attend this gathering.

Often, the owner would lose interest before the final finishes were put on their car and buy something else. Alternatively, some catastrophically expensive mechanical failure or a momentous crash would relegate the subject to a scrap yard before it was complete. There was the opposite end of the ownership spectrum also present, where the highly polished, concourse standard, classic cars abounded. For those with much deeper pockets than ours, the newer performance cars of the time were paraded too. This was the time of the RS Fords, VW Golf, Audi Quattro, Porsche 911 and BMW M3, these being a small sample of the many flamboyant and fast cars that were released in the mid-1980s.

This was the Southend-on-Sea Cruise on a Saturday night in June, 1986. Well, I think it was June; summertime anyway. Most of that year seemed to be summer in my memory. I was sixteen and mesmerised by the cars, the crowds, and the boys all driving their pride and joy. Before you say it, yes, they were all boys that I saw (sorry, I should probably say – young men). I can't remember seeing any female drivers, and I desperately wanted to be one, which felt like a very cool ambition to my mind, at that time. You gathered with the same faces, I was aware of people much older than us being there, however there was often sneering at the patched-up cars from those with the newer and more shiny ones. We stuck with our own.

I knew of this particular Capri driver; his name was Gary Curtis and he had just left my school in Billericay. He was one of the cool sixth-formers who had spent the last two years hanging out in the sixth form common room and not studying for his A levels. I knew also that he worked evenings and weekends at his dad's tyre shop. I had walked past often, trying to get a glimpse of him. I remember his floppy fringed, blond, streaked hair hanging over his eyes as he worked, shining under the fluorescent lights against the backdrop of oily dirt that coated the walls. I was a couple of school years below him and, as was the way of things, he didn't know I existed. His beloved Capri sat in the shop car park and on a Saturday, Gary's adhesive mates would gather there with their own cars, all in similar states of project ongoing. They would stay there all day, with their car bonnets up, tinkering. After the shop closed and Gary was released, they would all head to the Southend Cruise in convoy, joining others on the A127 Southend Arterial Road as they went.

The cars would group in the parking bays set into the middle of the wide two-way road along Southend seafront and take over the area between the pier and on past the Westcliff area. On this occasion, we were gathered adjacent to Peter Pan's playground, with the million coloured lights of this fairground beside the beach adding to the atmosphere. Screams drifted on the wind as the centrepiece 'Barracuda' ride rotated its two vast arms, with a rider carriage on each, in huge sweeping circles. The momentum of each arm appeared to pause momentarily at the highest point, suspending the people upside down for maximum screams, before accelerating back around its loop; its braking mechanism droning as it fought with gravity. Music from other rides blended with mechanical roar and the crashing of the bumper cars. Fairground diesel fumes mingled with popcorn, candy floss, chips and doughnuts and the ever-present baked seaweed smell of the estuary shoreline.

Slightly beyond Peter Pan's from our viewpoint, the mile-long pier stretched out far into the water. The pier was daintily lit by single white bulb strings, moving in the strong sea breeze; a contrast to the brashness of the brightly lit displays outside the amusement arcades such as 'Monte Carlo' and 'Mr B's' further along. These vast complexes competed for customers in the seafront row with pubs, chip shops, ice-cream vendors and a Wimpy bar. In the upper stories above, there were nightclubs, including the infamous TOTS (Talk of the South). The graceful architecture of the Grand Hotel resided up a steep slope, on the corner of the adjoining high street. It receded at night time, pushed into the darkness by the combined neon flare of the surroundings.

It was our world and the place to be on a Saturday night. The pavements were full of people, their faces alive with the evening atmosphere. The families with young children usually went home early evening and then the Saturday night older crowd came in. Driving to Southend for the Cruise, cars would come through the back roads of the town behind the high street, entering the seafront at the far end by the Kursaal building. There was often a lot of wheel-spinning around that particular roundabout, and it was later replaced by traffic lights to form a much calmer junction. Cars would then drive down the full length of the seafront with the arcades to their right and the sea on their left. They drove on, past the pier and Peter Pan's, to join the parked masses or to carry on up to the far end of the seafront where the road bends sharp right to go to Leigh or Westcliff. Alternatively, they would shortcut up past the

Cliffs Pavilion. Both routes would take you around Southend in a loop, which was often completed many times during the evening. It was inevitable that races often happened. The road was wide enough on the front in places to be side by side. The large police presence successfully deterred this in the main, however, the vastly outnumbered police couldn't be everywhere.

It was the time of tremendous sounds and not just loud engines with even louder exhausts. If you didn't have a particularly good car for the Cruise, 'that's cool' nods were often gained instead, by having a superb sound system in your car. Some extraordinary ingenuity went into shoehorning the biggest speakers into the smallest of cars, often sacrificing the rear seats and boot area to the cause. Standard fitment radio/cassette systems were discarded and dashboards cut about, in order to fit superior offerings from the like of Pioneer, JVC, Blaupunkt and Sony to play cassette tapes or even CDs, if you were really ahead of the game in 1986.

I watched Gary who had now parked the Capri in the centre parking bays and was standing alongside it next to his friends. One had a classic Mini Cooper in clean condition. Another friend had an older Escort RS2000 with similar filler splotches to Gary's Capri over its front end and the repairs to the rust on its wheel arches. The last car was a pristine white Escort RS Turbo with blue decals. I knew this last car to be only a year or so old, so presumed it unlikely to be owned by its driver who, like Gary, was eighteen maybe nineteen years old. Buffeted by crowds standing around the centre area, my friends and I ended up standing at the front of the Capri near the boys. I could hear the ticking of the Capri's cooling engine and tuned out my friend, who was gabbling excitedly while eating sugary hot doughnuts, in order to listen to the boys' conversation.

The white RS Turbo was indeed his dad's car it transpired as I eavesdropped. Dad worked for Ford in Dagenham and this was his company car. Much kudos to Dad for allowing it out of his sight to come here and be over revved to its red lines, I thought. I looked around while idly stroking the bonnet of Gary's Capri. The filler felt slightly uneven under my fingertips, with a granular texture that suggested recent work. In the next group along there were several Vauxhalls. I grinned to myself as I noticed they had been brightened by the addition of large decals or stickers on their side panels. This, in my opinion, was not cool. To buy the Halfords striping kit and emblazon the side of your car with the word 'TURBO' or 'INJECTION' in 12-inch-high lettering when your car clearly had no such thing on board was quite the sin against coolness.

Also 'not-cool' in my book: boot lid protectors that looked like the fingers of someone stuck inside the boot; anti-static rubber strips that hung to the ground from the rear of the car; too many extra spot lights; cheap self-adhesive window tinting; fake power bulges added to bonnets; dodgy plastic wheel trims pretending to be alloy wheels or, even worse still, painted in car matching colours.

Each to their own, I suppose, and we all had a love of cars in common at the time, despite wildly differing opinions regarding good taste. The Southend Cruise event grew out of nowhere by word of mouth, decades before social media, and continued into the next century. I loved going. It was exciting to watch all the cars and the people. Like most young people, I felt a powerful attraction to being on the edge of legality and pushing the social boundaries. From an older perspective now, some thirty-seven years later (gulp), I can appreciate that it wasn't universally loved. The Cruise was noisy, dangerous and often brought trouble that had to be policed and cleared up after. It was finished in this original form by the advent of speed cameras, dispersal orders and traffic calming measures in Southend in the following decades.

Oh yes, I nearly forgot to tell you! Gary noticed my hand on his car bonnet and yelled at me not to touch his car and to move away from it (or words to that effect, anyway). His mates and anyone within earshot all turned as one and stared at us, so we quickly beat a retreat into the crowd, glowing with embarrassment and completely crushed. I can remember the furious and aggressive look on his face to this day.

I was instantly cured of my adoration of Gary. however I kept my love of cars and especially those cars of the 1980s.

Little Ships Big Journey – By Wendy Ogilvie

Podcast title: A Strange Thing Happened on the Way to Dunkirk

Hi, my name is Ellen Ashdon. I've never done a podcast before but something strange, and very wonderful, happened to me and I wanted to share it.

The story I'm about to relate inspired the saying 'that Dunkirk spirit'. But it isn't just an historical news item for me, it's part of my history.

Just after midnight on 31 May 1940, six cockle boats from Leigh-on-Sea took their longest journey yet, to assist in the evacuation of over 338,000 soldiers who were under heavy fire on the beaches at Dunkirk. These 'Little Ships', as they were later coined, took part in Operation Dynamo along with over 700 privately owned vessels.

Sadly, not all the cockle boats and their crew made it home.

I first heard this story from my father when I was a little girl. My grandfather was one of the crew who took part in the rescue. I never thought much about it. At six years old, the most important thing in my life was ballet. It's now February 2022. The pandemic and my recent divorce have left me feeling lost at sea and very negative about life in general. So, I came home from London a few months ago to the comfort of my family and a new start.

I'm a history teacher by profession and my new appointment is at a local school. So, when my father reminded me of my grandfather's role in Operation Dynamo, I thought telling his story via a podcast would be a great way to get the kids interested in their local history.

On an early morning stroll with my father, I was relaying my idea about the podcast when he stopped and looked at me. His face, tanned and leathery, scrunched. 'What's a podcast?' he asked.

'It's like listening to the wireless in the olden days,' I told him.

He gave me a friendly nudge. 'You know what you need …?' he said, 'for yourself and your podcast.'

I shrugged.

'It was the eightieth anniversary of Operation Dynamo in 2020,' he said, 'but the pandemic meant we couldn't go through with the main remembrance celebration. So, this year, as many boats and crew as possible are going to attempt to sail to Dunkirk on the 31 May.'

'Dad, that sounds amazing!' I told him.

'There's going to be a ceremony when we get there. Obviously, we'll need the weather to be as fair as it was on that day back in 1940. Plus, we need to make repairs to the *Resolute*.' He stopped and raised his eyebrow at me. 'Are you in?'

At this point listeners, I wasn't exactly sure what he was asking me. Was he asking me to help with some light dusting of the boat's brightwork, or was he actually suggesting that I become part of his crew? I needed clarification. So, I said, 'You mean you want me to help rebuild the boat?'

'Yes,' he said with a laugh. 'We have a bunch of local volunteers including Archie and your uncle Richard, but it would be good if we could do this together.'

I still wasn't clear what he was asking so I tried again. 'But you don't want me to go with you?'

As I asked this, his face paused momentarily in thought before opening into a happy grin. 'That's a brilliant idea! Dad's son and granddaughter following in his footsteps. Or rather in his wake. You can record the whole event and put it on your wireless thingy.'

And that, dear listeners, is exactly what I did.

Here are some extracts from my diary entries. The full version is available in my three-part series.

6 March 2022

Working with natural materials is something my whole family is familiar with. My mum used to make her own woollen garments and sell them to exclusive boutiques in London. I'd never been into working with my hands. But we're now four weeks in and I can feel my shoulders have made some space for my earlobes at last. Is it working with wood? Working outdoors? Working with a group of people who try and cheer me up when I'm having a bad day? Maybe it's all of the above. Whatever it is, I'm grateful to be here and to have a reason for getting up in the morning.

15 April 2022

As I work on the boat, helping out where I can, my mind

doesn't go to the crap that's invaded my life. I'm just here, in the moment. At least that where I'm trying to be. I hear the sound of the water lapping against the sea wall and place my paintbrush on the tin before making my way outside.

The main body of the water looks almost motionless. Not unusual for this time of year. I inhale all the way to the top of my head, hold it and exhale, releasing any residual 'neggies' as my mum used to call them. Negative thoughts have been my constant companion over the last year; I even considered the unthinkable. But I'm slowly learning how to live for today.

I hear footsteps behind me and turn to see Archie approaching. He stands next to me looking out at the horizon. I wait for him to say something, but he doesn't so I look up at him.

'You know it's okay to just stand together and not talk,' he said, staring out at sea. 'You young people seem to have a need to fill every moment with sound. But sometimes it's good to stand side-by-side and take in the wonders of mother nature in silence.'

Archie took a long breath and dropped his shoulders, exhaling loudly. 'Let's hope she's good to us on Tuesday, eh?' He winked before turning back to the boat shed.

I'm realising that there is a sense of community that comes from taking on a project with others for a common cause. Maybe I could find real happiness again – someday.

Tuesday 31 May 2022

In the early hours, a small crowd gathered at the waterfront as we readied ourselves for the trip to Dunkirk.

My father gave a short speech before we left. He recounted the story of how Operation Dynamo came about

74

and why the cockle boats or 'bawleys', having broad beams and flat bottoms, were essential for getting closer to the beach. This would enable them to pick up the soldiers and transfer them to the larger boats further out.

The weather was on our side as myself, my father, Archie and Richard loaded the *Resolute* with essentials before setting off. I had never been to Dunkirk before and our boat and crew had never been further than Ramsgate. This was going to be an adventure.

The first hour went by with plenty of chat and excitement. Unfortunately, by the time we were halfway across, my sea legs had turned to jelly fish. I tried to ignore it by smiling and listening to Archie's many humorous stories of the sea. 'Concentrate on the horizon,' he said.

It didn't work.

We were due at to arrive at 15.00. As we got closer to the beaches of Dunkirk, my father began to explain what would have met his father and crew over eighty years ago.

'They could see Dunkirk from miles away as the flames and smoke rose from the shore,' he told us. 'We're lucky, we left during daylight but our cockle boats back in 1940 had to navigate unknown waters in the dark and without all the modern navigation equipment we have today...'

I watched the pride on my father's face as he spoke of those courageous men and their little vessels. But his voice was getting quieter; more distant. The boat hit a wave and my body heaved forward. The contents of my stomach wanted out! My eyes fixed on the front of the boat; following the bow up and down ... up and down. I felt myself sway forward and back ... forward and back ... forward and back.

A bead of sweat dripped into my right eye which felt weird as my face was devoid of any warm blood.

I tried meditating and took a deep breath. I could taste the salty air but it felt heavy entering my lungs. Then I saw it: the smoke and flames in the distance.

I turned to ask my father if this was part of the remembrance celebration but ... he was gone. In his place was a crew I had never seen before. They looked weary; their faces etched with concern. The light had faded and the sun was cloaked by a veil of smoke.

A loud *phwee* sound followed by a *boom* caused my body to stiffen. I looked up; a *rat-a-tat-tat* of bullets spat from a plane flying overhead.

What the hell is happening? Where's my father?

We were now much closer. The acrid smell of smoke hit my nostrils. I coughed as it travelled down my throat. The bitterness made me gag. The crew on my boat were shouting orders to each other. I watched as they scurried around reacting to the scene around them.

The captain, a stocky man in his forties with a moustache, was giving commands to the crew to prepare to take soldiers on board. It was then I recognised him; I had seen his picture every day over the last two months – it was my grandfather.

The smoke grew thicker. The sound of gunfire grew louder. I clamped myself to the edge of the boat; my protruding knuckles shaking with the tension.

Why am here? Is this hell?

We were almost at the beach. Surrounded by chaos. Hundreds of other boats began to appear, some large ships and others small like ours.

Still clinging to the side of the boat, I observed hundreds of soldiers; some scrambling out of the shelter of the dunes; some charging towards awaiting vessels ... towards hope. The electricity in the air was overwhelming.

The noise.

The chaos.

The fear.

This can't be real.

I covered my face with my hands and whispered a prayer. *I pray that sailors take refuge in You and also because You defend them ... Father let the praises...*

When I looked up the scene had changed.

A light beaming in front of me, expanding; obscuring the noise ... the chaos ... the fear. Until the darkness was gone. I turned my head to see my father looking down at me with one hand on my shoulder.

'Are you alright, love? We lost you there for a minute.'

I was no longer attached to the side of the boat but tucked into the well. We were still surrounded by other vessels large and small but the atmosphere was light and still. I could see groups of school children on the beach chattering.

'Come on Ellen.' My uncle Richard grabbed my hand and pulled me up. 'You'll feel better when we're on dry land.'

He was right, I did feel better once we were on the beach. The rest of the day was a wonderful experience where people of all ages and various nationalities told stories, gave speeches, cried, laughed and came together to remember a time and an extraordinary event.

So, listeners, what did happen to me out there? Did I really get a glimpse into what took place that day in Dunkirk? Was I dreaming? Or going nuts? Was the universe trying to give me hope in humanity? You tell me. I've heard stories like this one before called 'a glitch in the matrix' but I didn't believe it was really a thing until I experienced it.

Whatever happened, those men, including my grandfather, with their little ships and their big hearts, changed my life. If I'm honest, they *saved* my life. The experience of seeing those young men, and the civilians who risked their lives to bring them home, caused a permanent shift in me that has changed my whole attitude. One which I hope to pass on to my new students.

If you're listening and feeling adrift at sea, remember you're not alone and take solace from my story and inspiration from all those men and women who fought for us ... and for those six little cockle boats from Leigh-on-Sea who helped bring them home.

An Early Start – By Niall Palmer

Tap, tap, tap. The sound came suddenly, interrupting a dream where Ninian was frantically searching for his mother. For a moment, he didn't know where he was – if it was morning or night. He lay, heart pounding, willing his eyelids apart. Brushing the sleep from his eyes, Ninian began to focus on the objects in the room: a Victorian tallboy, his own iron-hard bed, and another smaller bed in the corner. Through the gloom, he could make out a pair of curtains, gapping just enough for the diffused light from a waning moon to steal through the glass, casting sinister shadows across something on the other bed; something that smelled of tobacco, whisky and woodsmoke. The sound came again. *Tap, tap, tap.*

The threadbare counterpane fell in a heap at Ninian's feet. Across the room, his gaze was drawn to a body, dead to the world. Rising to his not inconsiderable height, he staggered to the window, pulling back one piteously thin curtain. It had been an unseasonably cold Michaelmas, and the window was heavy with condensation. Wiping the damp away, in the street below, he could see a figure, lit by the lamp it carried through the fog: the knocker-upper.

Visits from this eerie, creeping figure came at a cost, but Ninian bore that cost stoically. Sixpence a week for tapping on his windowpane at five o'clock in the morning – sometimes earlier – to wake the sleeping dockers inside. Such was the way at the new Tilbury port – arrive late and lose the whole day's pay ... and Ninian could scarce afford to lose a brass farthing; the money was a good investment. He raised a hand to the glass; the figure motioned back. For a moment, Ninian would have sworn he saw his own face reflected in the lamplight and shuddered, before turning away as the figure drifted away into what little remained of the night.

Ninian's work clothes were already neatly laid out, ready for another day at Tilbury's great docks. As he picked up his shirt, he whispered so not to disturb the whole house.

'Magnus.' No response. 'Magnus, wake up. It's morning.' The shape didn't stir. He poked it with his foot. 'You can't be late again.' The shape shifted as Ninian fastened his shirt cuffs, and again as he felt the rough floorboards beneath his unbooted feet, struggling into his trousers. 'Magnus.'

'Leave me be. My 'ead 'urts.'

'Them that drinks from the devil's cup, shall never more be woken up.' Ninian tucked in his shirt and buttoned his braces. 'I shan't wait.'

He did wait of course. He waited, washing his face a second time at the nightstand, the smell of Lifebuoy Soap transporting him back to their mother's laundry in South Wales. He waited while he combed the knots from his tousled brown hair. He waited until the first light of dawn lifted the fog from a shade of coal black to a bruised green, yellow, and grey, until he could wait no longer.

Ninian's heavy-booted feet had barely reached the top of the landing, when a sturdy chestnut door, polished dark as mahogany by a century of blackened hands, creaked opened at the bottom of the stairwell. Ninian might have been startled had he not made out a familiar smile in the half-light of dawn – its remaining tooth as proud as an infant's first.

'Mornin', master Ninian.'

'Good morning, Mrs 'art.' He allowed his voice to sing freely now that the house was stirring. Mrs Hart had once described his Welsh baritone as 'melting wax dripping from a candle', so now, he always spoke a little more lyrically in her presence. ''Ow goes the day with you?' She seemed to shiver contentedly as he spoke, drawing her shawl a little tighter around her stooped shoulders.

'It's as cold a witch's teat! Even the knocker-upper must've rushed back to bed.' Her voice reminded Ninian of a terrier, in and out of foxholes, popping up inquisitorially whenever it found a scent. 'Course we never 'ad knocker-uppers till the docks came.'

'Idea come down from the factories in the north, see. Thank God for 'em I say – ships comin' in all hours nowadays.'

'Like young master Magnus.' Her words stung more than she'd probably intended, as the truth often does. Ninian's voice dropped to a bass-baritone.

'I must apologise for my brother. Rest assured we'll be 'avin' words.'

'Is 'e not workin' today?'

'Can't rouse 'im, see. 'E'll be the death of us both.' Ninian looked at his landlady, then cast his eyes down. Ninian had become the closest thing to family Mrs Hart had in Chadwell St Mary, and he knew that these tiny rituals – snatched moments on the stairs – had become the best parts of her day. He found it hard to hide his disappointment that Magnus had spoiled this one. She placed her hand on Ninian's arm. When he looked up, her eyes were still bright and kind, even though a redness spoke of broken sleep. Nothing more was to be said, though he fretted, nonetheless. Mrs Hart let both bedrooms in her terraced cottage to dock workers, while she slept downstairs. As far as Ninian knew, lodgers provided her only income, and at first, she'd seemed grateful for the few extra shillings Ninian's young brother provided. Lately though, Magnus had begun returning well past midnight, drunk, disturbing the whole house – even the half-deaf Mrs Hart. Ninian suspected the other lodgers had complained.

Ninian was still fretting about Magnus ten minutes later as he crossed from Chadwell Hill onto St Chad's Road. Nearing the turning for the docks, something caused him to look up. A sudden cold breeze, racing towards the river, lifted the fog just enough for him to make out an enormous twin-masted ship seeming to crack open the sky. It flew two flags: one red, one black. Then, just as suddenly, it was gone.

Later that morning, still troubled by his vision, Ninian was summoned by the dock foreman, Mr Murrell. For a moment, Ninian wondered if there was some truth in these old wives' tales about ill winds – but his fear abated as Mr Murrell announced 'Ninian Jenkins, I've decided to hang up my boots. I'm retiring.' Before Ninian could respond, Mr Murrell had offered him his job, with an increase in pay of six shillings a week. With one condition attached – his brother had to go.

At first, he considered refusing, mindful that he'd promised their mother he would always look after Magnus. Yet, by lunchtime, his brother had still not arrived. Other dockers were complaining that Magnus had been late numerous times and that his rope had no more slack to give, whether Ninian was foreman or not. Faced with the prospect of just one income to support them both, Ninian had no other choice than to accept Mr Murrell's offer. Six shillings extra would just cover their rent while Magnus found other work. So, Ninian reluctantly agreed to tell his brother, that night, that his services were no longer required at Tilbury Dock.

By the time Ninian returned home, it was already dark. Mrs Hart was waiting for him, her netted hair bobbing excitedly at the hallway door as he took off his boots.

'Master Ninian. Foreman at the docks!'

'Good news travels fast, Mrs 'art.'

'I've baked a rabbit pie. And there's leftover goose from Michaelmas. Still warm.'

'It smells delicious, but I must see my brother first.' She nodded as he handed her an envelope with their week's board and lodgings.

'Do come for some supper?'

He promised he would and took a breath before climbing the stairs. The door opened before he could even reach the handle. Magnus looked pitiful in the flickering light from his paraffin lamp, his eyes wet. 'I went t' dock. I already know, see.'

Ninian stepped towards his brother.

'You're to be foreman. Just like you wanted. Saint Ninian the Perfect.'

'I tried to wake you, Magnus.'

'You never tried 'ard enough.'

Ninian looked at his brother. 'There was nothing I could do this time.'

'Nothing you wanted to do.' Magnus stared blankly through the window into the late September night. 'I never stood a chance. Not 'yer, an' not with Ma neither.'

Ninian reached into his trouser pocket, pulling out two envelopes. 'Your wages. Las' week an' today. They didn' 'ave to.' He offered both envelopes to Magnus, before placing them down on his brother's bed. 'I put 'aff in yours and 'aff to post back to Mam in Ebbw Vale.'

'No point, see.'

'What's that to mean?'

'She's no use for money now.'

'Make some sense man. Has something 'appened?' Ninian's mind was suddenly a loom, trying to weave sense from his brother's words.

'I tried tellin' you but you never lissen.'

Ninian could feel a cold, prickling on his arms and neck. His legs felt weak. 'There's nothin' wrong with Ma. She's been sick, but she's gettin' better.'

'She got worse when you leff us. The doctor couldn't do nothin'.'

'We been sendin' money for medicine. You been postin' the letters.'

Magnus stared at his brother. 'That's why I come yer three month' ago. To tell yer. But I couldn't. You never stopped talkin' about 'er. Like she's a bloody saint.'

'I gave you money.' Ninian looked at Magnus helplessly. Magnus opened his mouth to speak, hesitated, then took both envelopes and stuffed them inside his coat. Ninian sat down on his bed. He heard his brother's steps descend the stairs and the front door open, then slam shut.

From the corner of his eye, Ninian noticed something small, sepia in the candlelight, poking out from under the mattress of Magnus's unmade bed. He recognised his own handwriting at once. An envelope, addressed to their mother, torn open. Inside, a letter had been removed, refolded, and replaced. The money was gone. He lifted the mattress. There, strewn about, a dozen opened envelopes, each addressed to their mother but never posted. Ninian snatched up his overcoat and strode out after his brother into the starless night.

Downstairs, Mrs Hart had heard one brother leave. Then, the other. A rabbit pie was carried to the pantry, uneaten. She'd fretted until the cold finally drove her to her makeshift bed. As St Mary's bell chimed midnight, she was still wide awake. All evening, her good ear had listened for the sound of one, or both, brothers returning. She thought she heard them once, but that was just a branch tap-tap-tapping against the window. Finally, just before one o'clock, she heard the front door unlatch and footsteps climb the stairs.

She couldn't tell which brother had returned. She waited for another set of steps to follow. An hour passed. Then another.

There was less than an inch of candle left by the time Mrs Hart poked her head out into the hallway. In the candlelight, she noticed a small pool of water on the floor, as if someone had stood, dripping after a torrential storm. Then, she thought she heard it again, ever so faintly, as if through water. *Tap, tap, tap.*

Upstairs, a damp figure lay shivering on his bed. Every time he closed his eyes, he could see those eyes bulging through the water, his brother's face hideously contorted. He decided he'd say they fought, that he acted in self-defence. Perhaps people might believe that, driven mad with guilt, or grief, Ninian had thrown himself into the dock. But what then? Even if he got away with it, he had no job. He couldn't stay here, and their mother would hardly welcome him back … God forbid she ever found out he'd let Ninian think she was dead in revenge for taking away his job. Then he heard it. *Tap, tap, tap.* It couldn't be five o'clock!

It came again. *Tap, tap, tap.* Magnus rose, moving toward

the window, ready to send the knocker-upper on to the next house. He looked down. A mist was rising. Barely a trace of moonlight. He strained his eyes, searching in the darkness. Perhaps the knocker-upper had seen him and moved on? Magnus turned back to the gloom of his bed.

Tap, tap, tap. The tapping came louder this time. He spun around, his eyes scanning the street below. Nothing. Suddenly, behind him, he heard something scuttle out on the landing.

Tap, tap, tap. Now, the sound was inside the house. Tapping against the door. He inched towards the doorhandle. Perhaps Mrs Hart had heard him moving around? As he reached for the doorhandle, it came again. *Tap, tap, tap.* He grasped the handle, breathed in, and opened the door, sure he would see someone, something, in the corridor – but nothing. Only darkness.

Tap, tap, tap. Now, the sound came from behind him. He swung around. *Tap, tap, tap.* Now it was coming from the walls. *Tap, tap, tap.* Now, the floorboards. Still the tapping grew ever louder. Now, it was coming from everywhere: the window, the ceiling, the tallboy. He hugged himself, wondering if this was some after-effect of too much whisky. But still the tapping would not stop. And now, it was inside his head.

Magnus turned back to the window, looking out, desperate to see someone. Anyone. Then, he saw it. In Through the gloom, a face – a swollen face, with bulging eyes – forming in the mist. A mist that now began to seep in between the window and its frame, slowly forming a human shape inside the room. As he watched, he could feel something tightening around his throat. He tried to get free, but it – whatever it was – was now more than a sound. It was a physical force, holding him. down. Now, it was inside the room. Magnus's final sensation was one of choking, gasping for air like a suffocating pike as he began to drown in his own blood.

He tried to call out, but he couldn't make a sound. As the blackness enveloped him, he felt his head crack against the wall, once, twice ... then everything went dark.

It was eight o'clock that morning when the town constable knocked on Mrs Hart's door. She was slow to answer, having been finally overtaken by sleep. A worker had found a body floating in the dock. The clothing was identified as Ninian's, though the face was bloated and unrecognisable. An ashen-faced Mrs Hart showed the constable upstairs, explaining that she'd heard someone return after midnight. There, beside an open window, they found Magnus. A doctor was called but nothing could be done.

Notices for the funerals of each brother were posted in St Mary's church, with the death knell tolled at evensong. 'Ninian Jenkins, taken by drowning'. Below, 'Magnus Jenkins, taken by three blows to the head.'

Tap. Tap. Tap.

The Sacred Quill – By Colin Payn

It is time for the ancient Contest again. And the 'Night of Peril' is tonight. Who will represent the two opposing forces and what will be their challenge?

Hilary, Joy and Alf are sitting in a quiet corner of The Crane pub, each sipping a non-alcoholic pint, and looking apprehensively at the list of ten possible contests drawn up by the two sides.

'I hope it isn't number five; November is no time to be swimming in the lake at Northlands Park.'

'Seven is worse, tightrope walking over open waste bins behind the Stacey's Corner shops.'

'Come on, you two, this is for the honour of the tribe.' Joy was fit, athletic and confident, unlike her fellow contestants. 'You did put your names forward, remember?'

'Oh, yes, like we had a choice. Well, we didn't. Because it's a family tradition. Hilary and me, the latest siblings in a long line of mouthy idiots who have ended up being chipped out of a block of ice, nearly spit roasted in a hundred-foot dash between burning trees and leaping over a dozen scythes wielded by blindfolded, laughing psychopaths.'

'That was all a long time ago. It's a lot safer now. They won't let you drown or break too many bones in the waste bins. We don't want to attract the attention of the public to our secret.'

Meanwhile, in The Winged Horse, three more faces were streaked with worry lines.

'Looking at this list I might have to pull a sicky,' Eileen's cold feet had started the moment her father guided her pen over the acceptance form, and now she felt her body shivering inside. 'After all, it's only a tradition, isn't it?'

The pub was warm and beery and loud, so Simon had to almost shout, 'Some of our forefathers died to secure The Sacred Quill, and you're snivelling over a little discomfort?'

'Shh, I know it's noisy, but don't say those words. And Eileen, only one of us will be chosen at the "Night of Peril" ceremony so you have better than even chance it won't be you.'

'I know, Sarah. What idiot in the 1920s decided that if women wanted equality, then it should apply to The Contest. Look at last year, running five times round the Eastmayne roundabout in a swimming costume without being killed.'

'It was on the roundabout, not in the road, and Alice did have a 100-yard start.' protested Sarah.

'Yeah, but who cares about a bloke in budgie smugglers? Whereas Alice had a car full of blokes going round and round with her, and only escaped when they were blocked by Nige in his Range Rover.'

'Perhaps a bikini wasn't the wisest choice, lots of white skin reflecting in the headlights.'

'Oh, I knew you would side with the blokes in the car, Simon. The Contest had to be called a draw, six months each to hold the … the prize.'

In 1363 The Contest resumed, after the scourge of The Black Death had wiped out any tribal rivalry but staying alive in the previous years.

The Doveidaas tribe of Fryerns had chosen their warrior and the name was dispatched by runner along the long winding Timberlog Lane, through forest and pasture, streams and clearings, until he reached the end where the tribe of Geldarii resided in the settlement of Vange. On the way, he met the messenger from Geldarii, and they stopped for a chat, complaining they could have exchanged messages halfway and saved a lot of hassle. But things had to be done correctly, according to tradition.

Tradition had a lot to answer for, especially the 'lost in the mists of time' version, of which The Sacred Quill was one. It was found, encased in amber, roughly halfway along Timberlog Lane and claimed by the leaders of both the Doveidaas and the Geldarii. It was revered based on the notion that it had been used to transcribe 'The Book of Wood' from the assumed original wooden version to vellum. However, as both had now perished, it was hard to determine whether The Sacred Quill might have smudged, and it should have been 'The Book of Word'. Nevertheless, both communities based their daily lives on what was remembered of The Book, through handed down verbal accounts.

The Contest that year was to kill a boar in the woods, single handed. This was doubly dangerous as the boar was fierce and could injure a hunter badly, and it was the Lord of the Manor's boar, death was the penalty for poaching. Tradition has it that the boar won, but The Sacred Quill went to the Doveidaas as their champion managed to get a spear into the animal, before spending the night in a tree to escape the tusks of the annoyed monster.

The coming of Basildon New Town posed a problem for the two tribes, who now had more secrets than the Masons, with the traditions confined to a few families on each side of Broadmayne dual carriageway. The Vange Geldarii family remained on what was left of Timberlog Lane, while the Fryerns Doveidaas family now had a renamed and widened road called Eastmayne laid over the top of their bit of Timberlog Lane.

The trees were gone but some open land remained, now privately owned by a large company for its sports ground; very handy for secret archery and horse racing. The contests continued with the families meeting in the two oldest pubs to be built in the new town, The Crane in Fryerns and The Winged Horse in Vange.

The danger of each Contest was toned down; nobody wanted to be seriously injured, and it always took place after dark to preserve the secrecy. Before Craylands was built, the land flooded every winter and stilt walking, marsh wallowing and ploughing matches were held there. Later, when Northlands Park was excavated and the lakes created, nighttime swimming contests were held in the freezing waters. Surprised night fishermen were bribed to stay silent with bottles of Newcastle Brown and cigarettes.

By the twenty-first century the traditions, handed down by word of mouth within each tribe, had been transcribed into a new 'Book of Wood', typed on a laptop unconnected to the internet and overseen by representatives from the Doveidaas and the Geldarii. Only two numbered, printed copies were made, and the laptop hard drive was destroyed. The copies are held by a prominent firm of solicitors and accessed by named representatives at the start of each year's Contest.

The 'Night of Peril' had been held in both camps, or rather

the homes of the two Grand Quill Masters. The unlucky contestants had been chosen, Alf to represent the Doveidaas, and Eileen for the Geldarii. Instead of exhausted messengers dashing back and forth between Fryerns and Vange to count the votes for which was to be the actual Contest, a Facebook poll had been devised so that all members could participate on the same night. It was a close race as the figures mounted, between the swimming, the dustbins and the eventual winner, the Sisyphus Challenge.

The chosen night was a Sunday, with good cloud cover forecast for the starting time of one o'clock. The venue was the pedestrian bridge that spanned Broadmayne between the school and the Craylands estate, the long spiral walkways at either end providing an ideal gradient for the task.

The time arrived and each end of the bridge was guarded from stray, inebriated walkers by several men in the traditional dark cloaks. The deep pockets containing Thermos flasks of coffee for the contestants and the watchers. The Grand Quill Masters walked up from either side, shook hands in the middle, which had been marked by a white chalk line, and continued on to observe the opposing side's contestant.

At one o'clock Alf and Eileen appeared, dressed in dark clothing but each with a knitted hat from which sprouted a single feather, representing the Quill. Mobile calls were exchanged to confirm their arrival, and a single, dog friendly, noiseless rocket announced the start.

Two heavy silver boules were placed at the bottom of each ramp and a cricket bat handed to each contestant, together with a head torch. The winner would be the first to get both boules over the chalk line at the centre of the bridge.

The bridge was old, the walking surface rutted, holed and matted with grass in places. A single hit of the boule could take it some way, but it often came back in a series of leaps from one rut to the next. Meanwhile, the second boule could disappear into a pothole, or roll back at surprising speed, bypassing the bat already stretched towards the first boule.

No words of warning were allowed from the spectators and, despite the coolness of the night, both contestants were soon sweating, having only covered about two yards up the incline.

The occasional car swept under the bridge, and a police car came fast through the roundabout with two tones blaring, blue flashes momentarily blinding the contestants who loudly cursed, while everybody else checked their pre-planned escape routes. But it was a false alarm, and the boules stopped rolling for no one.

By one thirty, Alf was ahead, having moved ten yards and approaching the first twist of the slope, when disaster struck. One boule bounced as he was about to hit it and rolled off into the darkness. Quickly corralling his second boule into a deep hole, Alf rushed down the slope, in time to see the now speeding silver globe take off the end of the tarmac and disappear into the long grass. Frantically scything the grass with his cricket bat, it took nearly five minutes to find the recalcitrant object, and another few minutes to get it back up alongside its partner.

Eileen had decided on a new tactic which consisted of whacking the boule as hard as she could in the hope it would bounce around the bend and stay there while she hammered the second one. But a heavy boule is not a cricket ball, and the big hits were wearing her down while only moving the damn thing about three yards before it started to roll back.

By two o'clock each contestant was given a short break to drink the coffee, the bat being laid across the walkway and the boules being held in position with horseshoes from an earlier Contest.

By three o'clock, neither side had reached the top and The Contest was abandoned by mutual agreement. Tape measures were produced, and the combined distance of the two boules from the starting point gave a narrow victory to Alf and the Doveidaas clan.

Another year over, Alf was given to singing, 'I am the champion', but only amongst family. Eileen moaned about her aching arms, but agreed it was better than falling in a bin full of restaurant waste. However, all agreed, after celebrating on the following two Saturdays, once in each pub, that traditions should be kept alive.

The reader may wonder if such ancient traditions are really still in existence. I would point to the celebrations of The Green Man, Wicca, Morris Dancing and many others too obscure to mention.

The reader may also wonder how I know so much about it, but I couldn't possibly say.

Aelfred's Tale – By Kevin Wood

A group of elders walked across the marshland towards Vange creek. They were to greet a boat of Kentish men approaching from the nearby river. The boat made its way from the river and onto the creek. Slowly propelled along the narrow waterway. The Vange elders took up a position by the muddy bank where the boat eventually moored.

Aelfred took a step forward as the men disembarked.

'Welcome travellers. Welcome to our settlement,' Aelfred said. He recognised the Kentish men as they had traded goods with them many times before.

In front of Aelfred was a tall, thick-set young man with dark wiry hair and a beard. He shook Aelfred's hand.

'I am Cadman, son of Gehdbert, from the Kentish settlement of Clofeshoch on the Hoo. I come from a high-ranking family. Our family are related to the Kings of Kent.' Cadman stood proudly in front of Aelfred and the other elders. He went on. 'Today I come to you Aelfred, not to sell my wares, as I and others have done many times before, but to ask you for the hand of your daughter, Cwen.'

Aelfred looked Cadman over as he finished his supplication.

'I welcome you Cadman,' Aelfred replied, 'as we have always welcomed you and your colleagues. We have always welcomed the goods that you trade with us. Nevertheless, I must make you aware that what you are asking of me is impossible. Cwen is already promised to Almond of Benflett, son of Aldhelm. His family is also well-appointed. Their pedigree is from the line of Cana. You no doubt have passed Cana's Island on your journey today. In addition, the union between Almond and Cwen will enable our two settlements to form an alliance that will bring peace to this land of the East Saxons.'

Cadman stared hard at Aelfred. 'I understand your reluctance. Yet I insist I will not be satisfied by this chastened response or the reasons that you gave. If needs be I will challenge this Almond for the fair maiden's hand.'

Aelfred's jaw tightened, he was annoyed at Cadman's response.

Cadman took a step closer to Aelfred and held his arm out close to his face, the hand clenched into a fist. 'I will have sweet Cwen with or without your approval, sir.' He waved his arm menacingly. 'I will return for her in seven days. If this Almond persists then he will have to fight me hand-to-hand for that right. First, I will take on Almond, then I will take my prize.'

'Cadman, you're behaving in a manner that shames your family,' Aelfred replied. 'Your people are also followers of the new religion. A religion that we have rejected. Cwen serves our Gods as we all do. This also makes any talk of your being wedded to her as an affront to those Gods.'

Cadman brushed away Aelfred's protestations with a wave of his hand. 'I will have your daughter. Prepare her, for when I return, I will take her back with me to the Hoo.'

Cadman turned and headed back to his boat.

Aelfred and the Vange elders remained passive as they stood their ground. The Kentish men boarded their boat and began their journey back to Kent. Both the elders and the sailors were left considering the undignified manner with which their meeting had ended.

Seven days passed. Aelfred had spent much of that time in discussion with Almond's father, Aldhelm. They had arranged for all able-bodied men from Vange and Benflett to assemble in the creek to meet Cadman and the Kentish men when they returned.

Almond spotted the boat first. 'There,' he called back to the others. 'Look there. They are heading towards Cana's Island.' Both communities came together at the same place in Vange creek where the elders had met Cadman a week earlier. As once again the boat made its way down the creek, the welcoming party waited for them by the bank.

The boat reached the bank and was moored in front of them. Cadman climbed out onto the marshland flanked by five other men who had sailed with him. He looked the waiting group up and down their ranks.

'We seem to have attracted quite a gathering of onlookers,' he said sneeringly. He turned to Aelfred standing close by. 'So old man I don't see Cwen here. Do you agree to my proposal or not?'

Aelfred looked down to the ground.

'I see,' Cadman said, inferring that this meant Aelfred didn't agree.

A younger man, a little way along from Aelfred stepped forward. 'I am Almond,' he said firmly, 'Cwen is promised to me. You will not have her.'

'And I suppose you've brought all your friends here for support,' Cadman said, waving his arm around at the crowd.

'I have my friends here from Benflett and my father.'

'Then we will fight for the hand of Cwen. But we will fight

hand to hand just the two of us,' Cadman said sneering at the onlookers as he did so.

Aelfred interrupted the exchange. 'Cadman, I have brought my friends and elders with me from Vange. They will ensure Cwen's welfare is considered and that the fight is fair.'

Cadman grunted dismissively at this. 'You are all in this together.' He turned his attention to Almond. 'Let's get on with this. I am impatient to win the hand of my Cwen.'

Almond shook his head at his insolent words. 'Then we shall begin.'

They squared up whilst the others that were gathered backed away. Both grabbed the others arms and made to wrestle their opponent onto the wet ground. They jostled like this until simultaneously they both fell onto the muddy marsh. They grappled back and forth, one trying get an advantage over the other. Cadman was the stronger fighter, but Almond had the better moves and fought smarter. Almond struck the first blow and his fist landed into Cadman's stomach. Cadman immediately responded with a salvo of punches to Almond's body and head. Almond spun Cadman over again. The battle shifted to another part of the marsh. The onlookers followed them across to keep watch. More punches and kicks landed as they rolled further into the wet marshland. Both men were now covered in wet and sticky mud.

Cadman attempted to get to his feet, only for Almond to grab his tunic and jerk him back to the ground. He twisted Cadman to one side and the blows continued from both fighters. Both men were bleeding from cuts inflicted by the other. Cadman's strength was beginning to overpower Almond, but Almond persisted.

Almond struggled to stand, but Cadman seized him and tried to pull his opponent back to the ground. Almond stood his ground but stumbled backwards. His left foot slipped into the muddy waters of a wet pit close by. Almond would have known of the dangers that the quicksand's in the marshes posed and withdrew his foot quickly. Cadman lunged at Almond, who side-stepped the lunge in the motion of removing his foot from the wet mud. Cadman's power thrust his body forward and passed Almond before plunging headfirst into the pit. He struggled for a moment whilst Almond, who had fallen backwards away from the hapless Cadman, steadied himself. Almond had found much safer ground nearby and dragged himself to his feet. Cadman was stuck in the muddy slime; he bobbed up briefly before finally disappearing to his watery death.

There was a moment of silence. The onlookers struggled to take in what they had just witnessed.

Cadman's cohorts ran forward to come to their comrade's assistance. It was too late. They tried to wade into the pit but had to be dragged out quickly. They knelt down and reached into the pit with their arms trying to feel for Cadman's stricken body. It was all to no avail.

One of the Vange elders approached them. 'It is no use,' he said, 'your friend has been consumed by the quicksand that is common on these marshes. You will not find any trace of him. His body has been taken by the spirits of the marsh.'

One of the Kentish men, from his kneeling position, looked up at the elder angrily. 'No!'

Almond was brushing himself down as his father walked over to him and checked his injuries. 'You fought well, Almond,' he said as his son continued straightening himself up. 'But the Gods were on your side too. You will make a fine husband for the beautiful young Cwen.'

The Kentish men had finally given up the search for Cadman. The one that had been kneeling down stormed over to where Aelfred was standing by the side of Almond and Aldhelm.

'You have not heard the last of this,' he said. He stared hard at Aelfred. 'I am Cadman's brother, Baldred. My father will be grief-stricken when he hears what has happened here today. My brother's death will be avenged. I will tell him and will vow to him that we will have a fair resolution, even if more blood has to be spilt.'

Baldred turned and joined his fellow ship-mates by their boat. As they began to row away one of them shouted back to Aelfred.

'We will return soon. We will bring others with us. You should be fearful when we do.'

Aelfred turned to Almond and his father. 'I fear this matter might not yet be resolved. I suspect the Kentish men may return as they say and wish to take this matter further.'

Aldhelm agreed.

Aelfred continued. 'Therefore, it is important that we conclude the wedding negotiations with all speed.'

'We already have many of the presents and oaths settled,' Aldhelm said.

Aelfred nodded. 'Let's try to resolve all the necessary remaining issues with a fresh urgency. I propose we assemble at the top of the hill between our two settlements. We will wed Almond and Cwen by sundown tomorrow.'

Aldhelm looked over to Almond who nodded his agreement. 'That is acceptable to us,' Aldhelm replied, 'we shall conclude the ceremonial requirements with you first thing in the morning.'

They shook hands. 'They will not come between us when they return,' Aldhelm said defiantly.

Aelfred agreed. 'We will stand together to defend our homes.'

Almond joined them as they clasped hands. The other men with them let out a loud cheer and chanted.

'We fight for the land of the East Saxons.'

PART TWO

In Part Two, various members of the Basildon Writers' Group took up the challenge to write a drabble to tell the world what Essex means to them.

So, what is a drabble?

Drabbles are very short stories, scenes or ideas which are usually exactly 100 words in length.

Sounds easy? Well, you may be surprised at how hard it can be to keep to the exact word count. There is an art in putting over an idea in so few words. Read on to see how our authors rose to the challenge.

Drabbles:

Rob Coke

Home Again

If a foreigner asked me where I was from, I'd say that I was British. But if a Britisher asked me, I would narrow that down to Essex. On my various travels across this country and others, that has always been the case. Sometimes, it is met with interest, and others, with a jest or two at the usual stereotypes. I have never lived anywhere else, but I do travel south of the Thames quite often, and one thing's for sure. Once I emerge back on the northern side of the Dartford Tunnel, I always feel like I'm home again.

Menderes Doğan

Meandering Through Essex

My name means meander in English. I was a wanderer all my life. For me, there were no clear-cut or simple routes. Now, I am meandering through Essex.

We don't have high mountains, long rivers, vast plains, or warm seas here, like the country I'm from. But it is much calmer and greener here in comparison to the city where I grew up.

Essex is special because I started my family here. Soon, Basildon will be the location where I have lived most continuously than any other place in my life. Thus, there must be something good keeping me here.

Jenny Drew

Essex Native

I adopted Essex.

Or did Essex adopt me?

It was a lot greener than the concrete jungle of South East London.

The accent is similar, if not the same.

Recent acquaintances ask if I am from Essex.

To which I reply: I am.

How long do you have to live somewhere before you can claim it as your own?

It's not quite been half my life that I've lived here.

But it's been a fair wedge.

Although I cannot claim to be an Essex native, or born and bred.

I can speak the lingo tickety boo.

I am from Essex!

Pagan Field

Home?

Belligerent cradle of birth – my home, I begrudgingly admit.

But there is beauty to be seen in the low, flat sprawling fields of glowing rapeseed; the steel grey shores of Southend-on-Sea; and time-forgotten villages just moments away from the micro-metropolises of Basildon and Billericay.

I am its crumbling pavements and war-torn roads; I am its bramble interlaced through hedgerows.

I am the endless parade of roundabouts; I am the future of a town in doubt.

Essex – mother, father, witness, stage and precursor of it all; my birth, my life, my happiness and sorrow.

Long may it triumph before the fall.

David Hawkins

Edges

Originally from the Midlands, I searched on the edges of the country and tried to find meaning. I found it.

I tried to find hope. I found it.

I tried to find love. I found it.

I found these three things in Essex and have stayed ever since. The shackles of my Midland accent have mostly dropped away. I can now speak Estuary English with the best of them.

Essex for me is not the place I was born, but the place I chose to be my home. I could not have made a better choice. I am happy here.

Lisa Horner

Not Essex Born but Essex Bred

Born in Enfield then flown to Australia at three months. I arrive in historic Colchester in 1968. I gain a brother, then it's on to Vange in Basildon as dad has got a job in Fords.

I try to eat salt dough bread rolls in nursery school, I make some friends. But before I really settle down, I'm whisked off to the village of Hockley. Our road has a field of horses at one end and rainbow puddles at the other.

Finally, my nomadic existence ends; I grow up in Essex. My well-spoken mother soon despairs at my lapsed consonants.

Janet Howson

My Town, My County

I can walk over the road to a tree lined park with colourful, carefully tended flower beds. Beside it, a wood, sun streaming through high branches with squirrels, deer, rabbits and woodpeckers to be seen.

Nearby, a buzzing town full of busy cafes with tables outside where friends and family meet. A short journey takes me to the estuary with walks along the promenade, a receding tide, a cooling wind, a smell of brine.

London is a short train ride away with its unparalleled history, art and theatre. Everything I love on hand. My town, my Brentwood, my Essex.

Dawn Knox

Familiarity Breeds Contempt – or Content?

Essex – the county of spectacular mountains, dramatic countryside, and beautiful beaches?

No. Not at all.

Essex is pleasant, mediocre, ordinary.

Some might even say dull.

I grew up in a town in Essex that in 1965 became part of Greater London, so I may have forfeited the right to be an 'Essex Girl'. However, I moved deeper into Essex as I grew up and have lived nowhere else.

I was educated here.

I met the love of my life and married here.

So, is Essex outstanding?

No, but it's the place that made me what I am.

It's my home.

GK Lomax

It's Where I Belong
I can do no better than call a poet to the stand. Kipling.

God gave all men all Earth to love,
But since our hearts are small,
Ordained for each one spot should prove,
Beloved over all.

For Kipling, it was Sussex. For me, Essex. Why? The land of the East Saxons boasts no towering mountains or majestic cathedrals. It's not storied in history. Its people aren't smarter, funnier or friendlier than those anywhere else.

It's just the place where I was born, grew up, have always lived. It's where I belong.

It's home – and there's no place like it.

Emma Marks

"Do you ever consider moving?"
It's OK, they know me here.
There's a lot to be said for that.
Familiarity and sentiment figure highly in my world and my soul.
In Essex, I see the places my family and friends lived in, worked in and enjoyed.
My roots, my stability, my history and future.
I feel no need to run from here, I haven't seen it all yet and it will keep changing.
Always more to explore.
Essex people are not easy to define, they surprise me often, good and bad and that's alright with me.
They are my people and I am at home.

Wendy Ogilvie

From Berlin to Basildon

From Berlin, in an army camp born,
To Rainham in Essex, a father to mourn,
From Rainham to Basildon, a new love I found,
Both, for my soulmate and the country surround,
From hidden pockets of park where we walk,
To kayaking along Paper Mill Lock,
From pretty villages where windmills stand tall,
To the coast at Southend, watching our dog chase a ball,
From the quaint buildings in Colchester, over 2000 years old,
To our modern libraries, where stories are told,
From the friends I have gained and the exploring I've done,
Essex is home.
Regrets? I have none.

Niall Palmer

At Home with the East Saxons

Three notched swords on a field of blood, each sod trodden by Germanic boots. We came from Europe, Suffolk, Danes and Celts, Asians, Africans, to melt into a rich genetic soup.

It's printed in my DNA; I'm one third Saxon stock. My family tree bedecked with Cunning Murrells, Farrows, Palmers, Everards. some riding pony carts from Poplar, some carried here – economic migrants in small boats. Coppers, poachers, noblemen, labourers. We're all a hybrid muddle, Essex folk.

A county made of ghosts, that generously gives us refugees, whether born or bred or merely passing through, a place we can call home.

Colin Payn

"I wish I lived in the countryside, like you."
A chance remark from a resident of East London made me reassess how I thought about living in Basildon. I had never regarded it as being countryside, it was our escape from London tenements to a rented, terraced house, our own front door, and a garden.

Urban man, perhaps that's me, from growing up in laid back cosmopolitan Hampstead, to the 1964 excitement of building site Basildon.

In reality, people are the key. Friends, relatives, clubs, voluntary organisations, the community. Essex is probably no better or worse than most counties, the challenge is with each individual, what can you contribute?

Kevin Wood

Essex - A Personal View

I moved to Essex in 1965. I have been defending the county against prejudice ever since.

I am based in Basildon. So my lived experience is mainly in South Essex. The people of Essex are not perfect. We argue with each other. We criticise things other people do, what they believe and how they behave... This doesn't make us odd. This is what people all over the country do as well.

I was born in North London, I've lived in the North of England, The Midlands and now in Essex. What does Essex mean to me? It is my home.

About the Authors

Rob Coke:

Rob is a very recent addition to the Basildon Writers' Group. Having been interested in creative writing for some time now, his interest in local and general history has inspired him to participate in this anthology. He is just starting his journey and welcoming the support and feedback from the other members of the group, encouraged by their knowledge to help improve his writing skills. Born in Basildon, Rob studied, works and lives locally and although at this time he is currently working on his first novel, the writings in this book are his first works to be published.

Menderes Doğan

Menderes Doğan was born in Turkey. He writes short stories in two languages: English and Turkish.

He has a degree in economics and worked in finance for a few years before moving to the UK. He works for the NHS and enjoys spending time with his family.

Menderes has a number of short stories on Turkish websites, online literary magazines, and national periodical literature magazines. He has some English short stories published in CaféLit Magazine. Many more English stories are still waiting to be edited or revisited, as he is not self-disciplined, even though he served in the army.

He has forgotten many things about the past, but he will always remember his secondary school teacher, who advised him to "never stop writing."

Jenny Drew

Jenny Drew is an avid reader of crime fiction and the odd occasional romance story. When she can tear herself away from reading her favourite crime authors and she stops procrastinating long enough, she enjoys writing crime fiction with a twist in the tale.

She plans to stop procrastinating long enough to write some more short stories and eventually, if she gets round to it, put them all together in a collection of short stories.

She very much enjoys being part of the Basildon Writers' Group and loves reading the diverse stories that come out of the very talented group of writers.

Pagan Field

Pagan Field is from Basildon and continues to live there, despite numerous attempts to escape. Pagan has a degree in English with creative writing, a masters in modern literature and a PCGE in English. She currently works as an editorial assistant for the *Health Service Journal (HSJ)* and is working on her debut novel, as well as a collection of horror stories. Pagan takes inspiration from such writers as Shirley Jackson, Carmen Maria Machado and Charles Bukowski. She hopes to one day retire to a cabin in the New Forest and dreams of adopting a pet crow called Mr Ruggles.

David Hawkins

David Hawkins was born in Birmingham. He is married and is recently retired, so he can now devote his life to finding new ways to avoid sitting down and writing his next novel.

His first novel was *Witness Protection,* a story about a man in Witness Protection trying to start a new life when he is still in the shadow of the old. His second novel was a coming-of-age novel *Something About Him.*

His third novel was *Hit and Run,* about a character who ends up bringing up the daughter of a girlfriend killed in a road accident. The next novel The *Two Husbands of Mollie*

Stevenson is an historical novel based in World War One, about two young men in love with the same woman when war begins.

Hector's Mess is about a secondary school teacher who finds himself in the middle of a murder investigation of a former pupil that is being investigated by another of his former pupils.

The Ghost Twin is a horror story that is also a human story. At one level it is the story of a twin haunting her sister after her mysterious, unexplained death, but it is also a story of family loss and how individuals cope with it.

His most recent novel, *Divorce and Other Disasters* is a dark comedy about a middle-aged man – Dave Bland – whose life spirals out of control after his wife divorces him and who then bounces from one crisis to another as he tries to find a new way to live his life.

David has written a children's novel called *Without Mum.* It's about Jenny, a ten-year-old who is suddenly orphaned and thrown into the care system where she has to find happiness for herself and her younger brother.

Find him at:
https://www.amazon.co.uk/kindle-dbs/entity/author/B00920J22K?_encoding=UTF8&offset=0&pageSize=12&s

Lisa Horner

Lisa is a published local history author. She was a researcher for the Basildon Heritage Project team and put together a blog which consisted of her research for the Basildon Heritage Trail, and information about it. She put this behind her when she went to university to complete an art and design degree. She was very surprised when Amberley Publishing got in touch with her, after viewing her blog, and asked her to write her first book, *Basildon Through Time* which was published in 2014. A few years later she wrote her second local history book, *Lost Basildon*. Lisa does find it a strange coincidence that she was born seventeen years after Basildon New Town came into existence, on the exact day, 4 January!

Lisa wants to use her creativity to write short fiction, perhaps endeavouring to write a novel one day when she is more practised as a creative writer.

You can follow Lisa on https://www.lisajhorner.com/.
Find Lisa's books on
https://www.amazon.co.uk/stores/author/B00PMAXOKY

Janet Howson

Janet Howson: After fleeing the North of England to the South for better weather, Janet was introduced to drama at a local theatre group. She progressed to teaching drama and English for thirty-five years in an assortment of comprehensive schools. That is how she landed in Essex. From a child, Janet was always an avid reader and writer of poetry. Then, during her teaching she wrote scripts for the pupils that were used for the school productions, once the familiar list of plays had been exhausted and she found herself directing Bugsy Malone for the third time. A long time later, retired and freer to pursue her interest, she joined two writing groups, one being the Basildon Writers' Group. The support she got from the groups encouraged her to write both short stories and books. She has three published books: *Charitable Thoughts, Dramatic Episodes* and *A Cue for Murder.* She also has featured in ten anthologies, one of them being *It Happened in Essex* the forerunner to this novel.

You can find Janet's books on Amazon books.

Dawn Knox

Dawn spent much of her childhood making up stories filled with romance, drama and excitement. She loved fairy tales, although if she cast herself as a character, she'd more likely have played the part of the Court Jester than the Princess. She didn't recognise it at the time, but she was searching for the emotional depth in the stories she read. It wasn't enough to be told the Prince loved the Princess, she wanted to know how he felt and to see him declare his love. She wanted to see the wedding. And so, she'd furnish her stories with those details.

Nowadays, she hopes to write books that will engage readers' passions. From poignant stories set during the First World War, to the zany antics of the inhabitants of the fictitious town of Basilwade; and from historical romances, to the fantasy adventures of a group of anthropomorphic animals led by a chicken with delusions of grandeur, she explores the richness and depth of human emotion.

A book by Dawn will offer laughter or tears – or anything in between, but if she touches your soul, she'll consider her job well done.

She has been a finalist in the Wishing Shelf Book Awards for 2017 and 2020, Readers' Favorite Book Awards 2018 and Independent Author Network Book of the Year Award 2018.

Dawn has written two plays about the Great War, which have been performed in England, Germany and France.

She has two historical romance sagas – The Lady Amelia Saga set in 18th Century New South Wales and The Heart of Plotlands, set in Dunton Plotlands.

You can follow her here on http://dawnknox.com and sign up for her newsletter for more information and free goodies.

On Facebook: http://www.facebook.com/DawnKnoxWriter
on Twitter: https://twitter.com/SunriseCalls

on Instagram: https://www.instagram.com/sunrisecalls/
on YouTube: https://youtube.com/@dawnknox1
on Amazon Author Central: https://www.amazon.co.uk/Dawn-Knox/e/B00JP64ZM4

GK Lomax

GK Lomax is a pseudonym. Behind it lies a rather strange individual, who mostly writes horror stories because he hates writing happy endings. He's been published in a number of anthologies, and even edited one once.

He's appeared on a number of TV quiz shows, was once cursed by Sean Connery for the errant nature of his golf, and sometimes thinks the end of the world can't come soon enough.

GKL is pronounced Jekyll. Go figure.

Emma Marks

Emma is part-way through writing her first novel around work commitments. She is a member of the Basildon Writers' Group and enjoys the encouragement and feedback. She has written several short stories for Writing Magazine and Brentwood Writers Circle competitions and has been placed 1st and 2nd for two of her submissions. She also wrote in the previous Basildon Writers Group anthology – *It Happened in Essex.*

Emma currently lives in Brentwood with her partner and two sons, and has lived and worked in Essex all of her life.

Wendy Ogilvie

Wendy has always been a writer but her main career was in the fitness industry as a personal trainer and course tutor for twenty-five years. She has written two fiction books: *Wandering on the Treadmill and Wandering Among the Stars,* both featuring a character called Wanda. She is now completing the first draft of a young adult thriller titled *The 36Club.*

She first began studying editing to improve her writing, and loved it so much she kept going! She is a member of the Chartered Institute of Editing and Proofreading and works freelance for established publishers and indie authors to ensure their prose are the best they can be before publishing.

Wendy lives in Basildon with her boyfriend, Carl, and their aptly named rescue dog, Rebel.

https://wendyogilvieeditorial.com/
Wendy Ogilvie - Author
Wendy Ogilvie LinkedIn

Niall Palmer

Niall Palmer grew up in Wickford in the 1970s. After a childhood spent ruining his dog's life by learning the violin, he eventually realised that ABBA was funkier than Albinoni, and quit classical music. He worked a trial shift in Adrian's Records on the High Street but wasn't asked back after mistaking Steely Dan for Steeleye Span.

With his career in tatters, Niall packed his bags and headed for the glittering lights of London. He began city life reading Scandinavian Studies at UCL, but quickly discovered that learning Old Norse was no guarantee of actually meeting Björn Ulvaeus. After a brief return to Westcliff, gaining his Equity card at the Palace Theatre, Niall boomeranged back to the big smoke, where he spent the next sixteen years lurking around Soho, Clapham, and a variety of West End theatres.

His work has been performed at RADA, the Jermyn Street Theatre in Piccadilly and Upstairs at the Gatehouse in Highgate. Niall, currently lives in South Woodham Ferrers, is writing a book of supernatural short stories, and studies Creative Writing with the Open University. He still hasn't met ABBA.

Colin Payn:

Before joining the Basildon Writers' Group, Colin had written many articles for travel magazines. The writers' group, however, gave him the confidence to realise his first novel, which had spent ten years in a drawer, might be worth publishing. *Dot's Legacy* https://mybook.to/DotsLegacy was published in 2016, followed by *Dot's Surprise* a year later, and the third book, *Dot's Secret*.in 2022

The trilogy follows the unusual, and sometimes bizarre, life of a modern couple who inherit a 'public' Park. Their benefactor, Aunt Dot, led an eventful, chaotic and entertaining life, but the Park is really a diverse and eccentric community, which it is the couple's true inheritance to maintain.

In between these books, Colin wrote short stories, many of which involved vehicles or travel. Putting them together evolved into *Transport of Dreams*, https://mybook.to/TransportofDreams a slim volume of stories ranging from the magical romance of a single journey around a *Carousel* in Honfleur, to the mature travellers in *Sex and the Single Camper*.

A complete departure in subject and writing took place when Colin teamed up with Dawn Knox, another member of the Basildon Writers' Group. Together, they produced a groundbreaking novel linking the two major world threats of Climate Change and Artificial Intelligence – *The Future Brokers* https://mybook.to/TheFutureBrokers Whilst living almost ten miles apart, the book was written and seamlessly edited line by line using Dropbox during the Covid lockdown. The result leads to the powerful conclusion that the biggest threat to mankind is mankind itself.

Recently, Colin has been working on various short stories and is planning a sequel to *The Future Brokers* with Dawn.

Find Colin's books on Amazon at: https://amzn.to/2ChlBkA
Website: colinpaynwriter.com

Kevin Wood

Kevin Wood was born in London in 1956. He lived in the North of England and the Midlands before coming to Basildon in South Essex at the age of nine.

He spent his working career as a Chartered Management Accountant before turning his hand to writing after taking early retirement. He writes dramatic dark thrillers, English urban noir, science fiction and climate fiction.

His first novella, a collection of short stories titled *The Search for Ellie Babble*, was published in 2022. It explores a number of issues in each story. Issues like abusive relationships, vengeance, mental health struggles and witchcraft.

He has had a number of short stories published on the website CaféLit Magazine. Two of these stories, "Isolation Day 1483" and "Pebbles on the Beach", were featured in the anthology *The Best of CaféLit 11*. This was also published in 2022.

The Search for Ellie Babble and the *Best of CaféLit 11* are available from Amazon books.

Printed in Great Britain
by Amazon